HASTY RETREAT

A Mother Lavinia Grey Mystery

Kate Gallison

Delacorte  **Press**

Published by
Delacorte Press
Bantam Doubleday Dell Publishing Group, Inc.
1540 Broadway
New York, New York 10036

Library of Congress Cataloging in Publication Data

Gallison, Kate.
    Hasty retreat : a Mother Lavinia Grey mystery / by Kate Gallison.
      p.   cm.
    ISBN 0-385-31896-0
    I. Title.
    PS3557.A414H37   1997
    813'.54—dc21   96-51547
                                              CIP

Manufactured in the United States of America
Published simultaneously in Canada

July 1997

10 9 8 7 6 5 4 3 2 1

BVG

Acknowledgments

For their kind acts of assistance and inspiration the author wishes to thank Susan Nadelson, Michael Buncher, David Rago, Brother Bede, Diane Bowman, and, of course, as always, Harold Dunn.

1

"An outward and visible sign of an inward and spiritual grace," said Deacon Deedee Gilchrist.

Recognizing a *Jeopardy!* question, Mother Lavinia Grey replied without thinking: "What is a sacrament?" She knew her catechism as well as the next person.

"Not in this case," said Deedee. "In this case the question is, 'What is mission furniture?' "

The two women were gazing into the cavernous library of the guesthouse of the Episcopal Monastery of St. Hugh. The library was furnished entirely with bookcases, tables, and chairs of a solid rectilinear appearance, the rich grain of their wood glowing in pools of light from curious square lamps. "Mission furniture?" Mother Grey said. "Is that what this is?"

"Mission in every sense of the word," said Deedee.

1

"Quarter-sawn fumed oak, outwardly and visibly gracious, though not, as you see, very graceful, strictly speaking."

"I think it looks fine," Mother Grey said. It was true that nothing she saw in there was overly decorated or curvy.

"Fine, yes, and perfectly apropos. Function without worldly frills, comfort without luxury. Just the thing for the weary spirit fleeing the fleshpots of late twentieth-century American society."

"Do they make this stuff specially for monasteries?" Mother Grey asked.

"No. It's old. It used to be made specially for self-righteous aesthetes. Then everybody wanted it, and after that it went out of fashion. Some old lady left this lot to the monks in her will, twenty or thirty years ago."

"It goes nicely here," Mother Grey said. "Show me the rest of the guesthouse." She was ready for the monastery experience. They had driven up here from New Jersey in Deedee's minivan, with a few of Mother Grey's parishioners, to make a Lenten retreat for the weekend. Deedee had talked her into it. The brochures looked good, and Deedee's own brother, Brother Fergus, was the prior. Deedee had lined up another monk, Brother Basil, a most devout and erudite old man, recently retired from a stint as a missionary in one of the hot spots of the Third World, to lead the retreat.

The very notion of holy monks, vowed to poverty and solitary contemplation, running a hotel, even a hotel of spartan accommodations and spiritual uplift, seemed almost contradictory to Mother Grey. All the same, no less holy a monk than Saint Benedict himself, founder of the Benedictine order, had recommended hospitality as a ministry.

It seemed to be working, on Mother Grey at least. Her first experience of the monastery guesthouse—the sound of rain on leaded-glass windows, the smooth cool feel of quarry tile underfoot, the sight of the many books cramming the mission bookcases—refreshed and pleased her. Her car sickness, engendered by the twists, turns, swoops, and dips of the final leg of their journey, was fading. She could see herself spending the weekend in one of these comfy (though never luxurious) morris chairs, reading, thinking, and recuperating from the stresses of pastoring St. Bede's, in Fishersville.

Brother Octavian, the brisk and preppy young guestmaster, had taken the others straight upstairs to their rooms to unpack and recover from the journey. Except for Deedee, none of Mother Grey's companions—not the elderly Delight van Buskirk, nor Martine Wellworth, nor fortyish newlyweds Annabelle and Roger Smartt—had ever been to the monastery before. It was a five-hour drive from Fishersville, interstates most of the way, with one stop for supper.

The Smartts, legally wed for a whole month now, had sat in the very back, where they whispered, giggled, and spooned like twenty-year-olds. Martine and Mrs. van Buskirk occupied the middle seat. While bits of knitting sprouted from Mrs. van Buskirk's clicking needles, Martine sat in silence, staring out at the nonscenery of the rainy interstate. It was some time before Mother Grey missed Martine's usual chatter, absorbed as she was in a struggle with Deedee over the aesthetic of the tape deck.

First Deedee played her tape of the Memphis Godly Stompers yodeling "Praise Jesus All You Out There." Mother Grey endured its cheerful bathos for half an hour and then replaced it with a more satisfying recording, Pablo Casals performing unaccompanied Bach sonatas and partitas.

A little dry for some, perhaps, but Mother Grey found it

altogether transporting; she shut her eyes and drifted into another dimension. After a tape and a half, Deedee called her back, declaring that she was sick to death of that stinking highbrow cello music.

Mother Grey countered that Deedee's white gospel tapes were mind-rotting trash.

"Martine," said Deedee. "Did you bring any black gospel tapes, by any chance?"

"Black gospel tapes?"

"Yes, the good stuff," said Mother Grey. "I don't suppose—" Actually, she didn't suppose. Martine wasn't the sort of down-home African American who went in for gospel. Indeed, Mother Grey hardly thought of her as a black person at all; if she pigeonholed Martine, it was as a yuppie lawyer. The way things worked out, this was a mistake, because Martine's race was important to Martine and also to certain others.

As to gospel tapes, however, Martine shook her head. "I guess I'm not that far into African-American culture," she said. "Maybe I should be. Which reminds me, Mother Vinnie, we need to have a talk."

"A talk?"

"Later on. I have something on my mind, and I need to unburden myself to you. As a friend." She handed up a cassette to them in the front seat. "Play this if you want to; I've already heard it." Martine's tape proved to be a recording of the latest legal thriller from John Grisham. But Deedee and Mother Grey wanted music.

A talk? So. Martine was brooding, and her bad mood had something to do with Mother Grey. *What did I do this time?* Never mind, she would find out soon enough. She set herself to searching for tunes.

She found nothing in the tote bag but more cello and some Isaac Stern.

"Unacceptable," said Deedee, handing her another tape. "Play this."

"No," said Mother Grey, handing it back. "No more New Christian praise songs." They rolled on in ill-tempered silence until at last she found another handful of cassettes under the maps in the glove compartment.

"What are these?"

"Something of Arthur's," said Deedee. The minivan belonged to Deedee's church, Holy Assumption in Ocean Prospect, of which the Reverend Canon Arthur Spelving, Deedee's boss, was the rector.

The cassettes proved to be recordings of plainsong, performed by Spanish monks. Divine. "Just the thing to set the mood for St. Hugh's," she said, and everyone agreed. But after they left the interstate, Mother Grey no longer cared about the music.

"It's the winding road," she mumbled, groping for a plastic bag. "Maybe we should stop for a minute." Fortunately they had arrived at their destination. Deedee nosed the minivan down the long wet gravel drive and into the monastery parking lot. Mother Grey got out, turned her face to the gently rainy sky, and took a deep breath of the piney woods.

Right away she felt better. When the others followed Brother Octavian upstairs to their rooms, Mother Grey was ready to go with Deedee to tour the rest of the guesthouse.

"So where are the other monks?"

"Let's see," said Deedee, whipping out her folded brochure with the schedule of offices. "Compline is just over."

"Evening prayer."

"Yes. They're back in their quarters, doing monk things. We'll see them tomorrow at matins."

"When can I meet your brother?"

"Later tomorrow. The Great Silence lasts from nine at

night to eight-fifteen in the morning. After that we can talk to Fergus." They passed through a shadowy hallway and came to a pair of big doors. "This is the refectory," Deedee said. Mother Grey pushed the door open and saw rows of dining tables, walls of rainy windows.

"What a view. That's the east bank of the Hudson, isn't it?"

"Yup. You'll love the food here."

"Of course I will," said Mother Grey. She loved almost any food prepared by persons other than herself.

"Brother Mortimer came here from the CIA," Deedee said.

"A spook?"

"A cook. The Culinary Institute of America is a famous chef school, right over there across the river. Brother Mortimer does all the cooking at St. Hugh's."

"You wonder about the past lives of monks," said Mother Grey. What would prompt a man to leave a good career and come here? Oh, yes, the love of God, certainly, but still, to withdraw completely from the world—

"You wonder, but it's rude to ask," said Deedee. "Let's go check out the sleeping accommodations. You have St. Cuthbert, I believe, and I'm in St. Anselm."

"St. Cuthbert?"

"The rooms are all named after saints. Come on up, I'll show you."

Sure enough, the glass transoms of the doors that lined both sides of the long upstairs hallway were painted with the names of saints. Over the door to the women's bathroom was the name of St. Dymphna.

"I'll see you later," said Deedee, and went to unpack.

St. Cuthbert was two doors farther on, a dear little room, painted stark white, with a narrow cot, a small chest of drawers, and over the chest an icon of the Blessed Mother with the Holy Child in her arms. On the wall beside the bed, a notice exhorted her to say a prayer, when it was time to leave, for the next person to stay there. She said one now for whoever had been there before her, and put her things into the drawers.

No one was in the library.

In one of the bookcases was a copy of *The Screwtape Letters*. The first time she had read it, she was fourteen—an interesting place in her life to wander back to. She took it from the shelf and went to find a place to sit.

There were many places, all pleasing if you liked oak. The stiff little armchair in the corner had a rush seat and a design of stylized leaves and stems, made of darker wood and two kinds of metal, worked into the central splat.

If this were mine, I would polish it, she thought. Part of the inlay looked like copper; a little Brasso would bring it up nicely. But of course she wouldn't polish it; she was a terrible housekeeper. She would merely think about polishing it. For sitting she preferred the chair next to it, no doubt an early recliner design, with pegs you could adjust to let the back recline. That one had leather cushions on the seat and back.

She adjusted the pegs to her liking, leaned back, and put her feet up on the oak and leather footstool. With a sigh of anticipation she opened the book.

But it was no good. Her attention would not be focused.

Deedee came in and sat in the chair beside her. "Something wrong?"

"Wrong?" Mother Grey asked.

"You're frowning and massaging your forehead."

"Oh."

"You came here to get away from it all, remember? To get some rest. Forget your personal life, forget diocesan politics, look for God in the wilderness and all that."

"What have you heard about diocesan politics?"

"Nothing you don't know already. I heard that the Archdeacon has left, and that your old friend Rupert Bingley is now in full charge of the Department of Missions."

"Rupert Bingley is an unregenerate blister."

"Didn't he save your life once?"

"Entirely by accident."

"What is it with you and Bingley, Vinnie? I've never heard you say a kind word about that poor man."

"That poor man is very powerful, Deedee, powerful well beyond the limits of his intelligence, and he wants to close my church."

"Why is that?"

"He wants my parishioners, he wants my windows, he doesn't think women should be priests."

"Your windows?"

"St. Bede's windows. You remember them, lovely English windows with angels and saints. The idea is to close St. Bede's and take the windows to St. Dinarius. One time he had the nerve to bring a carpenter to measure them. That was years ago, way before he became chairman of the Department of Missions. What is he going to do now? I shudder to think. His next attack could come at any moment."

"You'll beat him. You always have before."

"I open this book, and all I see is his smirking face."

"Forget him. You're on vacation."

"You're right." Away with all conflict, away with all strife. She would deliver her little flock into the hands of the excellent Brother Basil and find some peace and quiet. Next week would be plenty of time to gird her loins to do battle with Bingley.

Here came the flock now, the Smartts and Mrs. van Buskirk anyway. The Smartts were whining about not being allowed to sleep together.

"I thought we were supposed to have a double room," said Annabelle Smartt. She tugged at her knitted tunic. Was that a tunic or a very short dress? Were those tights or leggings? When Deedee had told them all to dress comfortably for the weekend, Mother Grey understood her to mean slacks and a sweater, not some getup that showed the dimples in one's knees. Mutton dressed up like lamb, Granny would have said.

Deedee tried to mollify them. "I'm sorry, but I couldn't get double rooms. When I called to make the reservations, the rooms with double beds were already taken."

"Who took them?" Roger Smartt said.

"The guestmaster said they were reserved for another group."

"What group?"

Mother Grey supposed Roger Smartt barked like that at his fellow employees at the software company, where he worked as some sort of middle manager. Here it was too loud, too strident. Even his false hair jarred. Normally Mother Grey didn't notice Roger's rug, but today the brilliant auburn hairpiece seemed to throb against the gray in his own hair.

"He didn't say. Some other people from New Jersey."

Who could have known that not sleeping together would be such a problem for the Smartts? Were they not there for prayer and contemplation? *A little self-denial never hurt anyone,* thought Mother Grey, who slept alone.

"You have all the time in the world," Delight van Buskirk pointed out. "Your whole lives."

"Some people consider it rude, you know, to enjoy conjugal bliss in a monastery full of holy celibate monks," Deedee said.

"Rude?" Roger said.

"Like eating in front of the starving." The Smartts exchanged a look, rolling their eyes at each other. Delight van Buskirk took out her knitting.

While everyone else settled down to read, knit, or contemplate, the Smartts put their raincoats back on and went outside into the wet dark—to have a smoke, they said. Maybe they planned to try enjoying conjugal bliss under a bush somewhere.

A few minutes of quiet, and then a commotion arose in the vestibule. Mother Grey put down her book and went to the door to see who was here. The new arrivals—perhaps the other group from New Jersey—were stamping slush off their feet, shaking their dripping umbrellas, and blowing on their hands.

There in the doorway, attacking his unruly umbrella with such zeal that he might have been trying to fold up the Devil himself and jam him into a nylon tube, stood bald, fat Father Rupert Bingley.

Of all the things he could have been doing this weekend, of all the places he could have gone, why this, why here? thought Mother Grey. *Pestilence.* There went her weekend of serenity.

Several of his flock from St. Dinarius were with him. What a waste of double rooms.

He looked up, and a slow horror dawned in his eyes as they met the horror in her own. "You!" he cried. Mrs. Bingley dug him sharply in the ribs, and he covered his discourtesy with a cough. "Ahem! Hem! Good evening, Mother Grey. What a pleasant surprise." A wife of the old school, Martha Bingley saw it as her duty to correct her husband's bad behavior. *Just as well, too, in Bingley's case,* Mother Grey thought. *Too bad she can't be with him all the time.*

"Father," she said. "How nice to see you."

Bingley seemed about to introduce her to the people he had brought with him. What would he have said? *People,*

this is my archenemy, the upstart priestess of Fishersville.
But Martha did the honors: "Mother Grey, may I present
Beryl Newmont."

A young woman with a dancer's body and a profusion of
curly yellow hair put out her hand. "Call me Berry."

"And this is her brother Jonathan"—a younger brother, a
slouching adolescent with pimples and a greasy hank of
straight hair falling in his eyes.

The boy tossed his head, temporarily clearing his view of
her. "H'lo," he said. "Smile," he said, and brought up a
palm-sized videocamera. Ugh! Technology in this holy
place! She gave him a frosty little rictus.

"I believe you know the Sedgewicks," Martha Bingley
went on.

My word! Rodman Sedgewick and his wife!

Mrs. Bingley was forestalled from making further intro-
ductions by Deedee, who put her rosy face in the vestibule
and announced in a stage whisper, "Nine o'clock, campers.
The Great Silence has begun." That was the last word any
of them spoke that night, at least in public.

Rodman Sedgewick. The last time she had seen Rodman
Sedgewick—just before she killed his chances for a seat in
the U.S. Senate—he had tried to whack her to death with a
polo mallet.

2

Even in deepest sleep Mother Grey's body, not well padded, was aware of the firm narrow bed. In her dreams she slipped back ten years to her honeymoon with Stephen, days on the trails making love in balsam groves and hiking, nights in the huts of the Appalachian Mountain Club. Separate sleeping bags, separate narrow bunks, four other hikers in the room snoring softly. In the darkness Stephen let his arm hang down, and she put her lips to his fingers, lightly callused from the violin, smelling of camp soap.

She awoke suddenly, alone, half-expecting to hear a hut attendant banging on a pan and bellowing the wake-up call. Dawn wasn't like the huts here; at six in the morning, the Great Silence was still in effect, and so nobody stood in the hall and banged and shouted.

A light knock sounded on the door of St. Cuthbert:

Deedee, keeping her promise to be sure that Mother Grey got up in time.

Matins was the first of the four offices chanted every day by the monastic choir of St. Hugh's; matins at six, diurnum at noon, vespers at five, and compline at seven-forty. It was all explained in the brochure. As Mother Grey recalled, the medieval monks used to turn out for seven offices, one of them in the middle of the night, can you imagine, but life was easier for monks nowadays. Or at least for these monks. Some monasteries still did all seven.

In the dark cool hallway at the bottom of the stairs, Mother Grey bumped into a slightly built monk hurrying to his prayers and almost knocked him down. His habit was black, denoting a novice, and so voluminous that even his face and hands were hidden. She nearly blurted out an apology, until she realized that the Great Silence was in force. How difficult it was to pursue normal social interactions under these conditions. He ducked his head between his thin shoulders and scuttled away.

What sort of fellows were these monks? That one seemed altogether furtive. Mother Grey and Deedee followed him until he turned aside at the chapel door and scuttled on down the hall. Deedee indicated with an elevation of her eyebrows and a nod of her head that this was the door by which the guests were meant to enter the chapel, and in they went.

Cool air smelling of candles touched their faces. Their feet whispered on the tile floor. Behind the altar the benches of the monks' choir faced each other; the visitors' hard benches faced the chancel. On the backs of the seats were racks holding hymnals and prayer books. Deedee and Mother Grey knelt and prayed, then thumbed through the prayer books looking for matins. Rustling noises announced the arrival of other guests.

At last, gliding like ghosts in their long white habits, the monks of St. Hugh's entered through a door behind the chancel and took their places in the choir. The little dark novice was with them. All their hoods were up, their hands in their sleeves; she could not see their faces.

In a high otherworldly voice, one monk began the chant. Then other voices joined him.

It was divine.

Afterward, as they made their way out of the chapel, Deedee gave her a little poke, as if to say, *Worth getting up for, wasn't it?* For the first time she noticed a sort of sculpture mounted on the wall, a cross made out of guns, some small, some large, some semiautomatic, all welded together and spray-painted black. The sight of it was shocking.

So, she thought, *the monks make political statements.* Not so unworldly after all. Bingley and his contingent glanced at the thing and moved on.

Not all of Bingley's people had gotten up in time for matins. Rodman Sedgewick and the lovely Beryl Newmont were nowhere in sight. For that matter, the Smartts weren't present either. Mother Grey hoped they could bring themselves to rise from their chaste and lonely beds in time for breakfast.

Still in silence, breakfast followed right after matins. Guests lined up to serve themselves from the buffet and then took their places at large plain tables. Mother Grey would not have called the cuisine modest. The food was much more varied and elegant than what she usually had for breakfast. Perhaps the monk who wrote the brochure had been rich when he was in the world, used to dining at the Ritz and the Pierre.

The monks sat apart from the guests; the little novice in his black habit was not with them. Perhaps they kept him totally cloistered for some reason.

In silence the working out of problems was done with the eyes and hands. When Father Rupert Bingley stepped on her toe in the course of pushing in line, Mother Grey tried to make furious eye contact, hoping at least for a nod of apology, but he stood with his back to her, piling pig-portions onto his plate.

She found a seat next to Deedee. Eating in company without speaking seemed strange—no small talk, no excusing oneself. Deedee tried a remark in American sign language—"Please pass the salt," it might have been—but Mother Grey's sign was too rusty. Anyway she was sure it was cheating. When they had finished eating, they bused their own plates—perhaps that was what the brochure meant by "modest"—and retired to the quiet shadowy library.

It was wonderful to sit and do nothing.

Perhaps not quite nothing. She resumed her reading of *The Screwtape Letters*. Again she was fourteen, thrilling to the spiritual insights of C. S. Lewis, safe in Granny's household, a small anachronism in the time of the hippies. Tea with Granny out of Spode teacups, embroidered tea cloth, cucumber sandwiches, bran muffins, banana bread. Long hours with her beloved cello. With this book in her hand—the very edition that Granny had given her for Christmas that year—she could almost smell her old room in the Georgetown row house, almost feel the hair of Fur Bear and Belinda, the toys that shared her bed. Certain modern theologians pooh-poohed much of what Lewis said as simplistic. But the young Vinnie had loved him, and the mature Vinnie found that she loved him still.

When she came back from a trip to the bathroom, Beryl Newmont was occupying her reclining chair, and Rupert Bingley had taken her book. Outrage caused her momentarily to forget the rule of silence: "Father Bingley! You have my book." People all over the library looked up and glared at her.

"No, no, my dear. I'm sure it's my book. A favorite of mine too, isn't it, Martha? Remarkably deep."

Martha smiled, nodded, reached over, and patted his hand. Martha was also sure the book was Rupert's. "Shh," she said.

Mother Grey actually considered for a moment retiring to her room and sulking. The transformation into her four-teen-year-old self must have been more complete than she knew. Instead she headed for the bookcases to try for another book. Delight van Buskirk beckoned to her from a chair in the opposite corner.

Mother Grey beamed at her and raised her eyebrows. The old lady smiled, patted the chair next to herself, and held out a skein of yarn, motioning to Mother Grey to hold it while she rolled it into a ball.

So Mother Grey settled back into yet another comfortable chair, put her feet up, and extended her hands with the yarn draped between them. From here she could drift into the past as easily as by reading a long-lost book.

Not into an easy place in the past, however. Knitting . . .

The feel and smell of the soft new wool brought back the days when she used to knit in hospital waiting rooms, wait-ing for Stephen to be tested, waiting for Stephen to be treated, waiting for Stephen to die. They had had less than a year together before he fell ill. After his death she had given all the sweaters away. Indeed she had abandoned housewifely arts altogether and gone at last in search of God.

In a sense she was searching still, but the Goal seemed nearer, especially in this quiet place. She moved her hands rhythmically to let the skein unwind. The yarn was a medi-tation. Presently she looked up and glanced around the library, checking out the people Bingley had brought with him.

Beryl Newmont, still in Mother Grey's favorite chair, wrote in a little notebook (prayerful observations, perhaps?) and darted occasional smoldering glances here and there around the room. It was the eyebrows. With such dark brows all one's glances appeared to smolder. Several times she seemed to be smoldering straight at Mother Grey herself. Sitting across from her, companionably, it appeared, was Rodman Sedgewick.

What was he doing here? Seeking enlightenment, or dragged along by his wife? Of all the unlikely candidates for a weekend retreat at a monastery! Once Mother Grey was sure she saw him smoldering back at Beryl Newmont.

Handsome in a coarse sort of way, Rodman Sedgewick was still an important man in politics, although his days of aspiring to the U.S. Senate were probably behind him, thanks to Mother Grey. *Or at least I hope I was partly responsible,* she thought. *He seemed to believe I was.* She had uncovered the misdeeds of his relatives, criminal acts so scandalous as to cause Sedgewick to want to keep himself and them out of the public eye. And so he worked behind the scenes, in politics and in law, and prospered as it seemed. His law firm had recently acquired the Newark law firm where Martine Wellworth was employed. All the same, though he appeared to enjoy the fruits of Protestant endeavor, nobody had ever accused him of being religious.

Suddenly the pen Berry Newmont was using dropped from her enameled fingers. With an elaborate show of searching for it, she crouched down on the cold tile floor and felt all around under the chair next to her. After a while she produced a small flashlight, directing its beam now at the floor and now at the chair bottom. Her head was all the way under the rush seat; Mother Grey feared she would get cobwebs in her yellow hair.

It was a strange performance. How far could the thing have rolled? At last she stood up, made a note in the notebook (using the now-recovered pen), and brushed off her clothes. The bell rang to signal the morning service of Holy Eucharist.

In a Tidewater Virginia accent like audible honey, Fergus preached a passionate sermon, as closely reasoned as a legal brief, denouncing the country's immigration policy. Inhumane and racist, he said. Rodman Sedgewick seemed to be squirming. Was Fergus directing the sermon at Sedgewick, with his rumored influence in Washington? Immigration seemed an odd thing to talk about here in the wilds of the Hudson River valley. Father Bingley was asleep.

Then the worshipers gathered around the altar and, in the style of the evangelicals, held their hands in the air to pray. The consecrated bread and wine had such a remarkably good flavor that Mother Grey actually noticed it. She wondered whether Mortimer was in charge of that too.

The services this morning were marked by a ceremony where the monks hung wooden crosses around the necks of three women, one of them Ouida Sedgewick. In the hall afterward, the Great Silence being at an end, Mother Grey asked Deedee what that was all about.

"They were being received into the Associates of the Holy Cross," Deedee said. "They must have mentioned this to you in seminary."

"Refresh my memory. What is it? The ladies' auxiliary?"

"Not quite. You practice the Rule of Saint Benedict, and after a six-month probation period, the monks hold a ceremony where they give you a cross."

"Ah."

"It's not just a club, you know, it's a whole discipline—
the balanced life of prayer, work, and study."

"Do you have to tend a garden?"

"It never hurts. Fergus! Come and meet my friend Vinnie
Grey." She waved to the prior as he came out of the chapel,
and he smiled and came over to them. Fergus towered over
his short plump sister, but in respects other than body
shape, they resembled each other; the family nose was unmistakable, while the family hair, thick and curly, had
turned the same shade of gray.

"Welcome to St. Hugh's, Vinnie. Brother Mortimer baked
muffins this morning," he said. "Better come along and
grab one. They don't last long."

"So Ouida Sedgewick belongs to the Associates of the
Holy Cross," Mother Grey said. "Does she come up here
often?"

"Does seem surprising," said Deedee.

"Perhaps you thought of her as the politician's wife," said
Fergus. "That's the role she plays in public. Ouida's spiritu-
ality is part of her private life. Yes, she comes here often,
has done for years. We're very pleased to have her among
the Associates."

Laid out on a counter in the refectory were coffee and the
loveliest muffins. Odd ceramic mugs hung on the wall over
the coffeepot, mugs that might have come from offices all
over the country, most with slogans on them: "World's Best
Grandpa." "Applied Data Research." "I have one nerve left,
and you're getting on it."

Fergus and Deedee served themselves and sat down at
one of the tables. Mother Grey took a mug that said "Sou-
venir of Santa Fe" and poured coffee for herself. Ouida
Sedgewick, newly adorned with the wooden pectoral cross,
appeared hovering at her elbow. She poured a mug for
Ouida too.

"Thank you," Ouida said. "Mother Grey, I wonder if we might talk."

Talk? "Certainly." What could this be? She hadn't seen Ouida to talk to in many months, not since the polo mallet incident. Was that what she wanted to discuss, after all this time? Or did she want to talk about Rodman's unhappy relatives?

"Let's go find a quiet corner," Mother Grey said. She left Deedee with Fergus and accompanied Ouida Sedgewick back to the library.

In nearly all the corners, groups of visiting young people were engaged in animated discussions of theology. Again Mother Grey was reminded of the AMC huts, where the animated discussions were of the trails, but no less passionate. Like the hikers, these people shared a unity of purpose, a feeling of being on the side of Right, of being different from the worldly.

She and Ouida found a private place almost behind a bookcase, with two chairs and a table for their coffee. Mother Grey waited. Ouida Sedgewick stared into her mug and fingered her cross. At last she spoke.

"Mother Grey, I know how you feel about my husband."

"You do?" Alas! Her feeling was that Rodman Sedgewick was one of the greatest rascals unhung, as Granny would have said, but she had hoped that nobody noticed how she felt, least of all the man's wife.

"Many women are attracted to him."

Attracted to him? To Rodman Sedgewick? As she looked into Ouida Sedgewick's face, her earnest fake little smile, Mother Grey wondered whether this birdlike woman was becoming unbalanced. *Attracted to Rodman Sedgewick? My word.* "I don't doubt that many women are attracted to him, Mrs. Sedgewick, but I can assure you I'm not one of them."

"It's something I'm quite used to, you see, silly women making a fuss over Rodman. But I must tell you, you need to know, that what Roddy and I have together—"

"Mrs. Sedgewick, your marriage will never be in any danger on my account."

"Oh, I know you think you're being discreet—"

"Will you please tell me what this is about?"

"You and Roddy."

"There is no me and Roddy. How can I put this without sounding rude? I haven't the smallest interest in your husband. The fact is that I cordially detest the man."

She dropped her eyes to her hands, folded in her lap. "I know that you came up here on purpose to meet him."

To meet him! "Mrs. Sedgewick, I came up here for a retreat. I did not come here to meet your husband or anyone else." *The woman has lost her wits.*

Ouida looked at her, eyes blue and wide, searching her face. Mother Grey pressed on. Perhaps she could reach her.

"Your husband—forgive me—is as repulsive an individual as I ever hope to meet. I hate pompous men. Had I known that he and the rest of you would be here, I would have rescheduled or called the whole thing off."

"Repulsive?"

"I'm sorry, I didn't mean to—but you must see, there is nothing between us. I did not come here to see him. I came here for some rest, and I'm not getting any, and it's just making me very unpleasant."

"Pompous?"

"Pompous, self-important, overbearing, fatheaded, dictatorial—"

"It's true that Roddy can be a little rigid sometimes."

"I know you're very fond of him, and I never would have said nasty things about him in front of you, but really."

Ouida Sedgewick bit her knuckle and stared into space, ruminating. "He came here to see someone."

"I've often wondered how you put up with him. If he's seeing other women, I must wonder all the more." Mother Grey stood up and thrust her fists into the pockets of her cardigan. Rich women made her tired. Freed of any economic need to struggle, Ouida had married Rodman Sedgewick in search of the requisite pain to know she was still alive. Or anyway that's how it looked to Mother Grey. Of course Ouida had no corner on painful men. She thought of Dave Dogg, the way he had looked the last time she saw him, the things he had said.

"I'm deeply in love with Rodman, Mother Grey."

Oh, yes, deeply in love. But you can't make a life out of that. "Chip and Lance are in college now, aren't they?"

"Yes."

"May I speak frankly? As a counselor. If you were one of my clients, I would tell you that you need to get out of the house."

"I do volunteer at the hospital once a week—"

"You need a job, Mrs. Sedgewick. Or you need to go back to school. Something that will absorb your energies. Clearly you are an intelligent and energetic woman. Don't you feel that you may have too much time on your hands?"

She considered this suggestion for a long time, plucking at the wooden cross around her neck. "Perhaps I could finish my master's thesis."

"What was your field?"

"Architecture. I was working toward a master's degree at the University of Minnesota when I met Roddy."

"You studied architecture, and you gave it up?" Incredible. What a waste.

"It was what one did. Then after a while Chip and Lance came along, and my life became, well, what it became."

"What was the topic of your dissertation?"

"The work of a nineteenth-century architect."

"What was his name?"

"Harvey Ellis."

A sudden crash, one of the ceramic mugs falling on the hard tile floor, was the first they knew that anyone was nearby. Coffee splashed and ran across the floor, pieces of mug bounced out from behind the bookcase. They looked up to see Berry Newmont, aghast at the mess, wringing her hands.

"I'm, like, so sorry," she said. She knelt down and began picking up sticky shards, placing them in a tissue in the palm of her hand.

Mother Grey bent over and picked up a couple of bits. "Let me help you."

"Don't cut yourselves," said Ouida Sedgewick. "I'll call Brother Mortimer." But he was there already, stout, smiling, carrying his broom and dustpan, plying his rag. In moments the mess was gone, and so was Brother Mortimer, still smiling.

"How does he do that?" Mother Grey asked, but Beryl Newmont was no longer there to answer.

"Things break here often," Ouida Sedgewick said. "He's used to it. The quarry tile floors, you know. The brothers don't want to use styrofoam cups because of the way they damage the environment generally. We bring a few extra mugs for the guesthouse every time we come up." She bit on a fingernail. "Tell me something. Do you know who that woman is?"

"Some parishioner of Father Bingley's, I think. Didn't she arrive with you?"

"She came in when we did, yes, she and her brother. But they didn't come in the car with us, and I'm not sure Father Bingley made the arrangements for her to stay here."

"You think she dealt directly with the guestmaster?"

"I'm not sure."

"She seems to know Rodman," said Mother Grey, thinking of the smoldering glances they appeared to be exchanging during the Great Silence. *Probably I imagined them,* she thought.

"Yes, doesn't she?" Ouida said, narrowing her eyes. "So you don't know her either."

"I can chat her up if you like," said Mother Grey. "Or would you rather I talked to Octavian?"

"Can you simply ask him whether Father Bingley brought her?"

"Why don't you ask Father Bingley?"

"I don't want to," Ouida said.

"Maybe you can tell me this, then," said Mother Grey. "Who is Harvey Ellis? Is there some reason why people should drop cups at the mention of his name?"

"Not that I know of. He was completely obscure, almost to the point of trying to cover his tracks, and then he died prematurely at fifty-two."

"Indeed."

"Researching his life and work was difficult because of the way he lived and worked. He would move from place to place, design things under false names, and let others take credit for his designs."

"But you chose to write about him. Why?"

"He fascinated me. In his way he was a great genius."

"How were you able to find out anything about him at all? How did you even hear about him?"

"I became interested in his work while I was studying at the University of Minnesota," Ouida said. "Some of his drawings are in the Buffington archives. The old Federal building in St. Paul is mostly his work, a lovely thing, more or less in the Romanesque style of H. H. Richardson and yet with the loveliest proportions. They were going to tear it down in 1971, but a local group bought it from the federal government and restored it. Now it's called the Landmark Center, and it's used as a museum. Try to see it if you're ever in St. Paul."

"Okay," Mother Grey said. "Are many of his other buildings still standing?"

"No, not many. There are some in Rochester. His papers are there too, in the hands of what's left of his family. He was in business with his brothers in Rochester for a while, but most of their work is gone." She sighed. "Urban renewal."

"So after you and Rodman were married, you abandoned your work on Harvey Ellis."

"Yes. That was so long ago! Since then other scholars have become interested in Harvey Ellis, and I understand that he's better known than he used to be." She sighed again and settled back in her chair, then suddenly leaned forward and glanced nervously around the room, looking no doubt for Rodman Sedgewick, the man who had supplanted the joys of scholarship in her life.

"Whatever made you think that your husband was coming here to meet a woman?"

"I overheard part of a telephone conversation."

"I think you must have put the wrong construction on it."

"I hope so. I know I'm pathologically jealous. I pray about it all the time. But you know what they say—even paranoids have enemies."

"It's as I told you. You need to get out of the house."

"You're right. It's why I'm here. Actually it was I who insisted that Roddy come here this weekend."

Here was the explanation for the presence of Rodman Sedgewick, no monk and no holy man, at St. Hugh's. Ouida, insanely jealous, wouldn't let him stay behind.

"Then how was it that you thought we had arranged to meet?"

"You could have followed him up here."

Yes, she was completely insane. "Put the whole idea out of your mind. I have no designs on him whatever."

Ouida Sedgewick frowned, turning things over in her mind. "Fatheaded?"

Mother Grey seized her by the hand. "I tell you what. Let's forget we ever had this conversation. I'll forget you accused me of chasing your husband, and you forget the things I said about him."

3

In the quiet front hall, Octavian was manning the registration desk, not that there was any traffic, but the records seemed to be in need of updating. The clerical side of a mission of hospitality.

Mother Grey greeted him and said she had a question to ask him. He smiled at her, playing with his pen. She noticed his hands; his nails were rough, his fingers stained, his palms too callused for a mere contemplative.

"What do you do here when you aren't being guestmaster? Besides the prayers and offices, I mean."

"I make furniture," he said. "Was that your question?"

"Actually, no," she said. "It's—this is sort of silly—Ouida Sedgewick sent me to find out whether that blond-haired girl signed up to come here this weekend herself, or whether she was registered by Father Bingley to be with his group."

"Gosh," said Octavian.

"You know the one I mean, right? Her name is Beryl Newmont."

"She came with Father Bingley's group, she and her brother. How would Mrs. Sedgewick not know this?"

Mother Grey was embarrassed. How did she get into these things? "I don't know," she said, as much to herself as to him. "What sort of furniture do you make?"

"Honest furniture," he said, with a strange proud grin.

The phrase was meaningless to her, but she smiled and nodded as though she knew what he meant. "See you later," she said, and went away. The idea had a whiff of New Age hippie heresy to it, the morality of inanimate objects. It rather reminded her of Deedee's assertions about the mission furniture, that it was made for self-righteous aesthetes. She tried to picture a piece of dishonest furniture. Okay, first of all it would be crooked. Then, if it was a chair, it would fall down when you sat on it, perhaps, or if it was a table, it would teeter.

Honest furniture. He didn't mean holy furniture, either; that would be something else—carved chairs for visiting bishops to sit in, pulpits, pews, and the like. The market for church furnishings was not what it had been a hundred years before; on the contrary, the way the churches were closing right and left, there was surely a glut.

The bell rang for lunch, interrupting these ruminations. Later, Mother Grey could never remember what they ate, although she recalled being favorably impressed. The fleshpots had lost an excellent chef the day that Mortimer took his vows.

What probably knocked the bill of fare from her mind was the confrontation with Martine Wellworth in the library afterward. She was sitting reading, digesting her excellent lunch, when Martine came and sat down in the chair next to hers.

"Mother Vinnie, I need to talk to you about something that's bothering me."

"What's wrong?"

"It's about Mac."

"Mac Barrow?"

"You're seeing a lot of him these days."

"Yes, quite a bit of him. He's an awfully nice man."

"Mother Vinnie, I wonder . . . I wonder if you've thought this through."

"Thought what through?" What was to think through? A pleasant man, handsome too—Mac could have passed for Denzel Washington, one of whose movies she had rented after several people pointed out the resemblance. Every now and then Mac asked her to go out to dinner with him, or a concert, and once he got hold of a pair of tickets to *Tosca* at the Met. (Was it significant that the diva was black? The question had never crossed her mind before.) Mac Barrow was an excellent organist-choirmaster, the first one at St. Bede's since Mother Grey had become vicar there. Next week would mark the end of the six-month trial period, during which he had insisted on working for nothing, repairing the hundred-year-old organ, training three of the parishioners to sing. Luckily he had other sources of income. She would have to find the money to pay him now, for she couldn't bear to let him go.

Martine was nervously rubbing the top of her pen on the arm of the chair, oblivious to the gouge she was digging in the grain of the wood. Mother Grey seized her hand in both of hers and held it. "What is it, Martine?"

"Mother Vinnie, this is painful for me to say. I wouldn't

bring it up at all, except that I like you so much, and my not talking about it is poisoning our friendship."

"My word."

Martine put her free hand on top of Mother Grey's hand; they might have been choosing up ball teams, using the pen for a bat. She looked Mother Grey in the eye and said, "I don't think it's appropriate for you to be dating an African American."

Mother Grey was stunned. When she got her breath, she said, "Why not?" Not that they were dating. Mac Barrow was not courting her. They had interests in common, they enjoyed each other's company, they were friends.

Martine launched into a long and deeply felt disquisition on the history of Africans in America, ranging from the abuses of slavery and segregation to the present unhappy tendency of inner-city black males to shoot each other to death. *Black males,* Mother Grey thought irrelevantly. *Why black males? I guess it's racially offensive to call them boys, and yet so many of them are too young to be called men.*

Her own mother worked herself into an early grave, said Martine, to give her children a chance at an education. And for what? They get out into society, and all they encounter is a wall of racism. "Your friend Rodman Sedgewick is a drooling racist, by the way. None of the African Americans in the firm will ever make partner, now that he's in charge."

"Martine, Rodman Sedgewick is no friend of mine, you must know that. What does all this have to do with me and Mac?"

"It's just how I feel. I'm sorry."

Mother Grey had no idea, at short notice, how to respond to this. That Martine should meddle in her social life, either as a parishioner or as a friend, was an intolerable intrusion. But could she point this out without losing her temper and further alienating Martine? At last she said the stupidest thing she could have said: "Thank you for sharing." Martine glared at her and left the room without a word.

Mother Grey closed her book with a sigh. Racism. She reflected on the big dustup about racism at the last two diocesan conventions. She had concluded, after all was said and done, that no two people meant the same thing when they said "racism." When the bishop, for instance, said, "Stamp out racism," he meant for the white people to become pure in their hearts and sensitive to the dignity and equality of their African-American brothers and sisters. When the Caucus of Black Episcopalians said, "Stamp out racism," they meant, "Give us good jobs, give us money to run our parishes, give us political influence in the diocese, and after that you can worry about your hearts."

Staircase insights presented themselves as soon as Martine was out of sight. *Wait a minute. Wait a minute. I'm not supposed to date Mac Barrow because . . . because Martine is getting passed over for a partnership?* But she was gone. Mother Grey would get her thoughts in order and talk to Martine later, if Martine would talk to her ever again. Was this political or personal? Good heavens, could Martine be thinking of dumping Albert, her faithful if stodgy husband of seven years, father of the excellent Henry, and making a play for Mac?

No, probably Martine simply meant what she said, which was that it made her uncomfortable to see black men going out with white women, even her friends.

Deedee came in and sat down in the chair Martine had vacated. "Look at that," she said. "Somebody put a gouge in this nice old piece of mission oak."

"I just had a fight with Martine."

"About what?"

"She thinks Mac Barrow and I are an item, and it offends her."

"Why?"

"Because he's black."

"My, my. And are you? An item?"

"Actually, no."

"You sure?"

"He's in love with St. Bede's Hook and Hastings tracker organ."

"You should marry Dave Dogg," Deedee said for the fortieth time. "That will put an end to all this talk."

Why was it offensive for Martine to advise her to stop seeing Mac, but not for Deedee to advise her to marry Dave? *My word, am I a racist too?* Or was it that Martine's advice was negative, Deedee's positive?

Ah, the hell with it. "I can't say that I'm ready to be serious about either one of them," she said.

"Too bad," said Deedee. "I was rather looking forward to their fighting over you." She waved the book of Sherlock Holmes stories she was holding. "Rather like Holmes and Moriarty at the Reichenbach Falls. Except on the Fishersville wingdam instead. The mighty waters of the Delaware swirl around their ankles . . . they grapple in a titanic struggle . . . in the end nothing remains for the faithful Watson but a terse note."

"Who gets to be Watson?"

"You do."

"I don't see myself as Watson. Anyway, if I remember that story, neither Holmes nor Moriarty came back. Holmes himself disappeared afterward for many months."

"Exactly," said Deedee. "So tell me, should I read *The Final Problem* again, or abandon Sherlock Holmes and go for Butler's *Lives of the Saints*?"

"*Lives of the Saints* is considered more uplifting." *Racism, racism.* "Deedee, have you noticed that none of the monks here is black?"

"Why in the world would a black man come all the way out in these woods to take vows of poverty?"

Father Rupert Bingley, rector of St. Dinarius, who had never taken vows of poverty and never would, was seeking muffins in the refectory. Brother Octavian stood by the coffeepot.

"It seems to be a busy weekend here," Father Bingley said to him.

"It is," said the guestmaster. "Besides your people and the group from St. Bede's, we have the Youth Fellowship Club with us from California. They're on a bicycle tour, and they're spending the night in tents out on the grounds."

"Wonderful. And in this weather too."

"They say it will be warmer and drier tonight," Octavian said. Bingley found himself wondering what this personable young man, with his decent haircut and his good boating shoes, was doing here at the edge of the earth, in this outpost of the godly. He should have been tending a wife and three children in some civilized town like Darien, Connecticut.

On the other hand, maybe this was the last place a devout Wasp man could go to be free. Bingley thought, *Maybe we've been pushed out of every other niche of American society by minorities and women.*

His Department of Missions was to meet on Monday, he reflected. One woman at least would get pushed in return when that meeting took place, if Father Bingley had anything to say about it. It was time for Mother Lavinia Grey to release her death grip on St. Bede's.

China. She should go to China. The Lord would surely find a use for her there.

"Do you know each other?" Octavian asked. "Brother Basil, this is Father Rupert Bingley from Rolling Hills.

Brother Basil has just returned from Africa. He was more or less driven out by the recent unrest."

"How do you do," said Basil, in an accent distinctly British. Remarkably firm handshake for such an old man. He must be Church of England. They knew how to deal with women priests. *Or do they? Let me see. They just held some kind of a vote there.*

Africa?

"How do you do," said Father Bingley. Yes, she should go to Africa. A fertile field for a woman of Mother Grey's energies. Perhaps Father Bingley could get the bishop to agree.

Sedgewick came in with an empty mug. "I don't believe you've met Rodman Sedgewick," Father Bingley said to the monks.

Sedgewick nodded to them as he poured himself more coffee. "Interesting sermon," he said to Brother Fergus. "Although perhaps more appropriate for a soapbox than a pulpit."

"You don't believe in immigration reform?" Fergus said, smiling.

"Oh, yes. But immigration reform is the business of the legislative body. I believe in the separation of Church and State."

"I do too," Fergus said. "The government should have no established religion. This is not to say that Christians in public life ought to behave like heathens. You're the chairman of the Committee to Restrict Alien Privilege, aren't you?"

Sedgewick puffed himself up and began to spout his views on immigration. "Foreigners are taking jobs away from our own citizens, Brother Fergus. Bleeding us white. The country is being overrun. You people here are cloistered, but if you saw more of the world, you'd notice. Asians, Africans, Hispanics, pouring over the borders. Every town in New Jersey has them now, hanging on street corners and jabbering in foreign tongues. Hardworking middle-class families have to pay to send the children of illegal aliens to school."

"Children who don't go to school can become very troublesome adults," Fergus said. "The cost to society of dumping the children on the streets would be much higher than the cost of educating them, don't you think?" Father Bingley realized suddenly that Fergus was lobbying Rodman Sedgewick.

"Send them back where they came from," Sedgewick said. "Or put them in detention camps. Lock them up until they can give a good account of themselves. Some of these people are nothing but terrorists."

That seemed reasonable to Father Bingley, but Octavian disagreed. "To me that sounds almost like thinly disguised racism," he said. "Our country was built by the efforts of immigrants. What they need is more education, not less." So these monks were liberals, Father Bingley mused. Could they influence Sedgewick's views? Evidently not; Sedgewick gave a snort and turned his back on them, unwilling to engage them in political debate. It was then that he came face to face with Brother Basil, and their eyes met.

The old man smiled and greeted him: "Rodman. How are you?"

Sedgewick's mouth fell open.

"It's Brother Basil," the old man prompted. "I taught you calculus at St. Botolph's in Zurich. Remember me?"

The encounter with his old teacher almost seemed to upset Rodman Sedgewick. If he didn't know better, if he didn't half-suspect that Sedgewick feared neither God nor man, Father Bingley could have sworn that Basil made him nervous, the way he was blushing and scuffing his feet. But whatever the strange quality might be of the ongoing social interactions, the way was now clear at least to the coffee and muffins, as Octavian and Fergus swept out of the room, habits flapping.

Thinking of awkwardness reminded Father Bingley of Lavinia Grey. No sooner had he thought of her than here she came, with her fat little friend, the odious Deacon Gilchrist. He took a muffin and buttered it, poised for escape.

Sedgewick recovered himself. "Of course I remember you, sir. I'm flattered that you remember me," he said. Father Bingley edged away from the coffee counter. The women were bearing down on him.

Basil said, "Certainly I remember you, Rodman. How could I forget? You were the first student at St. Botolph's of your—"

With a weird spastic gesture, Sedgewick knocked over his cup, spilling hot coffee on the monk's white robe. A number of other mugs crashed to the floor.

"I'm so sorry," he said. Father Bingley was suprised at Sedgewick's confusion. How long ago had Sedgewick been in school? Thirty, forty years? It gave one pause, the effect that a confrontation with his former self could have on a man.

"Quite all right," said Brother Basil. "I'll just go put this to soak." He hobbled out.

As Father Bingley fled after him, he heard Deacon Gilchrist say, "Nothing worse than a dirty habit." This sort of facetious remark was one of the many reasons why that woman would never be allowed to become a priest. Not while Father Bingley had any power to prevent it, at any rate.

He nearly collided with Brother Mortimer, who came smiling out of the kitchen with his broom. Presently the sounds of broken crockery being swept up into a tin dustpan echoed through the hall.

* * *

Mother Grey was relieved to see that Brother Basil's habit was clean and dry when he emerged from the monks' quarters and into the room where he was to lead her group in their spiritual reflections. He must have had a spare.

Basil's excellent life and qualities were well known to Mother Grey, at least as far as Deedee was aware of them. She had bent Mother Grey's ear for hours about the elderly monk's virtues. Truly he was a remarkable man, a missionary who had trolled for souls for Christ in the four corners of the world, a scholar who had written and published ten books, a singer who still possessed the remains of a fine baritone voice, and an ordained priest (as were many of the brothers). Still, as he talked, Mother Grey allowed her mind to wander back to Fishersville and the blue eyes of Dave Dogg—relaxing her vigilance over her flock from St. Bede's. She thought it was only for an instant, but when she came to, they were asking Basil about his personal life.

"Why be a monk? Why withdraw from the world? What do you people do with yourselves?" they were asking him.

He described the life of the monks, their concerns, what they gave up, what they prayed for, what they longed for, how they spent their time. He showed them his new shoes, suede brogans, and confessed that he actually owned two pairs now. Still, he had needed Fergus's permission to buy the second pair. His other shoes were open sandals. He had worn them in Liberia, but they were unsuitable for the winter weather here in New York State.

He revealed that the brothers at St. Hugh's had a television set, and that they kept close tabs on events in the world. On Mondays, when the guesthouse was closed, they sometimes took the monastery truck and drove to New York City.

New York City. What did they do there? *Perhaps,* she thought, *they get their hair cut.*

Annabelle Smartt fired off the final burning question: "Why is it that the women's bathroom is named after a saint, while the men's has no name at all?"

"You'll have to ask Brother Fergus," said Basil. "The rooms were named before my time here. It may have to do with the fact that this was once a boys' school, and in those days there was no need for a women's bathroom on the second floor. One of the sleeping chambers was probably converted for that purpose." He stood up; their hour with him was over. Mother Grey vowed to herself that she would remain alert during Sunday's session and steer the talk into something more spiritual.

Deedee looked out the window and announced that the clouds had all gone away. "Put on your coat, and let's go explore the grounds," she said.

The sun was indeed out, but the evidence of last night's storm still lingered in icy puddles. The going underfoot was tricky. They started off on a flagstone path that wandered over a hill to the guest parking lot, stuffed with church vans. Some of these vehicles must have belonged to the support team for the youth group cyclists. Then they struck off through the woods, making a wide loop toward the river, and came across the field where the young folks had pitched their tents. From there they worked back along the river side of the monastery.

If there was an herb garden in the manner of Brother Cadfael's little patch, they did not come across it. Perhaps it was behind the wall that sealed off the cloistered parts. Just before this wall a shed roof projected from the side of the monks' quarters, and under the roof wide flat boards were stacked with mathematical precision, shims holding them apart so that air could circulate around each board. They might almost have come from the same great oak tree. The smell was sharp. "Hardwood," Deedee muttered. "They're curing it."

"Must be for Octavian's honest furniture," said Mother Grey. They followed a path away from the building, across the weedy lawn, and down through the bushes.

"What was Ouida Sedgewick carrying on about this morning?" Deedee asked.

"Rodman. She thinks his latest flame followed him up here."

"Oh?"

"Worse. She thinks it's me."

"Ha! Ha!" Deedee roared. "You and that stuffed shirt! As though you could love a man who attacked you with polo mallets." She wiped her eyes. "He has no inner core of self." It was Deedee's vilest insult.

"Ouida doesn't know about the polo mallet thing. I mean, she walked in on us, yes, but she misunderstood what was happening." They came out of the bushes onto the muddy bank of the Hudson. Sunlight sparkled on the broad water; a mile away they could see the east bank.

"All of which reminds me," Deedee said. "I think Sedgewick is hitting on that blonde, Berry Newmont, and not with polo mallets."

Mother Grey shushed her; Berry's little brother Jonathan was lounging against a tree ahead of them, squinting out over the glistening water through the viewfinder of his videocamera. As they came quietly up behind him, they heard him inhale sharply and hold his breath. *Asthma medicine*, Mother Grey thought. *Must be the pollen here.*

But it wasn't that; he was smoking a joint.

Wouldn't the smoke spoil his picture? Youth. In another few years she would probably hear that Jonathan Newmont was directing pictures in Hollywood, forming the minds of the young who came after him.

They worked their way along the bank for a few hundred yards until Mother Grey found a seat on a dry log. "These people are Rupert Bingley's parishioners, not mine," she said, as much to herself as to Deedee. "I have no more interest in interfering with his parishioners than he has in interfering with the way I run St. Bede's. Considerably less, if I'm not mistaken."

"Still, I think Sedgewick and Berry are playing footsie," said Deedee, and sat down beside her.

"Don't be ordinary, Deedee."

"Hmf. You call that ordinary, you who watch *True Stories of Real Cops* as a daily obsession, on the very television set that you bought so you could see *The Choir* on Masterpiece Theater. Why do you do that, by the way?"

"It's because of Dave."

"Dave Dogg wants you to watch *True Stories of Real Cops*?"

"He doesn't know I watch it. I keep thinking it will give me a handle on him, help me understand why he is the way he is."

"Tcha. If you want to understand him, you should ask him to explain himself. That's my advice. Or are you not speaking again?"

"Oh, yes. Yes, we're speaking. That's one of the reasons why I was so anxious to get out of Fishersville for the weekend." She picked up a stone and threw it far out on the water. It skipped twice. "Between the problems I have at home, the hot pants of the Smartts, and Sedgewick and his women, I'm beginning to think this wretched retreat is about nothing but sex."

"Dear me."

"Hot pants in the sense of their breath, I mean, of course."

"Of course."

"On the other hand, it might be about mission furniture."

"I was hoping you'd get something more spiritual out of it," said Deedee.

"Martine thinks it's about race relations. She's going to straighten me out."

Deedee got up. "Actually, Vinnie, it's about God. It's about reconciliation, it's about putting things in the Lord's hands and letting Him take care of them."

Mother Grey got up and put her hands deep in her pockets. Here was Deedee preaching at her, a thing that she found annoying. It seemed to her that when there was preaching to be done, she ought to be doing it herself, not suffering it from Deedee. "My favorite part of it is the quiet," she said.

"Okay," Deedee said, and after that she was quiet. They went back inside. It was time for vespers.

4

Talking was still allowed at supper, which came after vespers. Deedee seemed withdrawn until Mother Grey apologized to her for biting her head off. Deedee accepted the apology with good grace and cheered up a bit, but did not seem to be her old bubbly self. *Should I pursue it? Should I badger her to tell me what's wrong?*

Maybe later. Dinner was calling.

Another meal prepared by hands other than mine, Mother Grey thought with pleasure. The sumptuous menu, the friendly appearance of the monks in their long white robes, the young folks deep in spiritual discussion; how easy it was to forget the adversities of Fishersville and simply wallow in good feelings.

Bingley was still here, of course, but look at it this way: as long as he was here, he wasn't in Trenton campaigning to close her church. He sat with the brothers at dinner to-night, perhaps to talk of spiritual matters, but more proba-bly to avoid Martha's wifely scrutiny of his diet. Relaxing at last, Mother Grey gazed at him almost fondly.

The monks, if Mother Grey but knew it, were discussing not spiritual matters but temporal. Fergus spent the entire meal urging Father Bingley to put the bite on Rodman Sedgewick for a large donation to the monastery.

"You can't really mean you're short of funds," Bingley said to Fergus. Really, it was hard enough to pry donations from Sedgewick for St. Dinarius itself, his own home par-ish, let alone for some distant religious community of sig-nificance only to the man's wife. Let them hit her up for donations.

"St. Hugh's is always short of funds," Fergus said. "The building requires constant upkeep, and even a community vowed to poverty has to eat and clothe itself."

"When I returned to this country, I was shocked, shocked, at the price of shoes," Brother Basil said.

"If things continue the way they're going, St. Hugh's may not survive into the twenty-first century," Octavian said.

"Some of us might have to go back out into the world," Basil said. "Our little community of prayer and contempla-tion will be gone forever."

"That is, unless some innovative way is found to raise money," said Octavian dreamily. He seemed to have some-thing in mind, but he didn't say what.

The others all turned to look at Rodman Sedgewick, the richest man in the room.

"Let's go talk to him," said Basil, taking Father Bingley by the arm. "He was my student years ago, did you know that? I taught him mathematics."

They cornered the Sedgewicks as they were clearing

their plates. Brother Basil opened the conversation: "I meant to ask you, Rodman. How is your dear mother?"

"Mother has been gone for many years now, Brother Basil."

"Pity. A wonderful woman. So courageous."

"Yes," said Rodman Sedgewick. But rather than stick around so that Basil could open the real subject at hand, Sedgewick put his plate on the pile of plates and bolted, shoving Father Bingley in his haste.

As Sedgewick passed through the crowd, Bingley could hear Ouida: "Brother Basil knew your mother?"

"He taught mathematics at St. Botolph's."

"But Roddy, I thought your mother died when you were born."

"Of course. Of course she did," said Sedgewick. "Basil has me confused with one of his other students. He's an old man, and I'm humoring him."

"Really."

"Yes, really."

Mother Grey also witnessed this odd exchange. Talking to Basil made Sedgewick so jittery that she almost expected him to throw his crockery on the floor again. What was it about Sedgewick's mother?

She was tempted to approach Brother Basil behind Sedgewick's back and ask him. But she did not. Later, of course, she was to kick herself.

The monastery was so quiet, the regular repetition of prayer services so steady, that a deep feeling of peace stole into Mother Grey's soul. They went to compline and listened to the ethereal voices of the chanting monks, asking God to care for them through the night. Then it was nine o'clock, and the Great Silence began once more.

A long day. Mother Grey's narrow cot began to call to

her. Among the uplifting biographies of saints and C. S. Lewis tomes in the bookcases, she found a lone paperback whodunit. She took it to bed and read it for a while, until thoughts of Fishersville and the parish of St. Bede's came crowding in.

She put the book down on the floor beside her cot—there was no nightstand, nightstands were worldly—and thought about Rupert Bingley. Perhaps it was time she swallowed her old resentments and tried to make friends with him, if only for the sake of her parish. Otherwise he was sure to recommend disbanding St. Bede's altogether at Monday's meeting of the Department of Missions; he couldn't see the use of it, he had told her many times; he felt that her little patch could be adequately covered by St. Dinarius, his own church. He was even willing to send a van for her congregation.

St. Bede's was very vulnerable now. Not only did her enemy, Father Bingley, have great influence in the Department of Missions, but Mother Grey herself was in bad odor with them. For though as a mission church St. Bede's accepted money from the diocese, they were obliged to give money to the diocese as well. This they had not done.

There was none to give. Plate offerings were falling off, pledges were not being honored. Parishioners with jobs were leaving town. Plenty of reason to lie awake, maybe even feel panicky.

There were mornings when she came into the sanctuary, lit the candles, looked out at the tiny congregation, and thought, *In a little while perhaps this will no longer be a holy space.* Like many another church it could easily be closed, sold, deconsecrated. Father Bingley would take away the windows. Many were the antique dealers who would love to open a shop there.

She hated the idea. This was her church, her very first

parish assignment, and though the late Bishop Wealle had sent her some years before to gracefully close it—"Take three months, if you need them," he said—yet in her stubbornness she had hung on and was hanging on still. St. Bede's was a beautiful church. It had stood in Fishersville through storm, rain, and flood for a hundred years. The windows, with their delicate angels and saints, came all the way from England.

And it wasn't only the building that was worth saving. The Church had a mission in Fishersville among the dispossessed, the alcoholics, the addicts, the homeless people who lived on the fringes of Fishersville's yuppie prosperity. If she abandoned them, as Dave had asked her to do again the night before she left on this retreat, she would leave an enormous despairing hole. Never mind that no one came to church. Never mind that no one gave her money. Fishersville needed her. She explained this to him, yet again.

"But even the diocese wants you out," he said.

"I don't want to go."

In answer to that he had kissed her, a kiss that she could still feel on her mouth. It was a very good argument but not decisive.

And to think that Martine resented her friendship with Mac Barrow! Mac was the least of her romantic concerns. It would not be Mother Lavinia Grey who took that handsome and eligible African-American bachelor out of the mating market.

As for St. Bede's, the Lord would take care of it according to His own purposes. For now she would sleep.

As her eyes fluttered shut, the noises began.

She heard them as if in a dream, flapping slippers, squeaking bedsprings, muffled thumps. She did not get up to see what might be going on but drifted deeper into sleep. Here in this holy place of contemplation, what could be amiss in the depths of night? They were all in God's hands. Probably the sounds were of the wretched Bingley attempting to relieve a well-earned bout of indigestion.

But in fact Father Rupert Bingley was not suffering indigestion at that hour, which must have been sometime around midnight, he reckoned. He was suffering hunger.

Half an hour earlier he had been almost asleep, but just as he felt himself slipping over the edge into oblivion, his wife had spoken to him: "Rupert, did you ever consider a monastic vocation?" The sound of her voice startled him, and after that the sense of her words. A monastic vocation.

"I can't remember," he told her. What a strange idea, coming from his wife, after forty years of marriage and three children. When they were married, the Church had been a rock for a godly man to found his career on. Who could have foreseen the way it would crumble and change? What if, instead of marrying Martha, he had holed in, donned a long white robe, and spent the last forty years with these monks in prayer and silence?

No diocesan politics. No late-night demands from needy parishioners. No worries about money.

No colicky babies, no burned roasts, no critical in-laws, no wayward teenagers, no college tuition. No grandchildren. No sweet Martha sharing his bed all these years.

Would he have gotten to Heaven any faster?

"I don't think so," he said to her. "I would have missed you too much." She was asleep.

Between his churning thoughts and the shuffling and rustling noises in the hall, Father Bingley was wide awake now. He lay on his back, his whole professional life passing before his eyes. It was good, his professional life. He was pleased with it. He wasn't bishop, of course, nor even an honorary canon, but his influence at the diocesan level was satisfying, and his salary as rector of St. Dinarius was ample. He flattered himself that he had brought a number of souls to Christ. Taking a leaf from Mother Grey's book, he had even managed to do some good works in the community. His day care center was doing very well. If he were to die tomorrow, he could give a good account of himself before his Maker.

Martha would miss him, of course, and even with all he had achieved, there was still more to be done—the building fund, the outreach program. No, no, it was not time to go yet. He thought fleetingly of the results of his most recent physical exam, the admonitions of his doctor, then quickly put them out of his mind.

How soundly his wife was sleeping. Her gray hair glinted in the light that filtered through the frosted glass of the door to St. Arbuthnot; her shoulder rose and fell gently with her soft breath. A sweet woman, a wonderful helpmeet. No, he would not have wanted the life of a monk.

What he wanted was a snack.

He got up, slipped into his baggy white terrycloth robe, and pattered down the hall. He remembered seeing a bowl of fruit in the refectory. A banana would hit the spot. On his way to the stairs, he was startled to smell a whiff of smoke, not the smoke of burning buildings nor yet of pipes and cigarettes, but something almost medicinal.

It was coming from St. Sebastian, young Jonathan's room. Marijuana?

Father Bingley opened the door to speak to the boy, forgetting again about the Great Silence. The light was on, making visible the pungent layers of smoke that floated in the room. No one was there. The narrow bed was rumpled but empty.

For an instant he thought the miserable child must have

driven himself berserk with drug use and rushed off to commit some atrocity in another part of the monastery. But no, people didn't really do that—his daughter had explained that to him. More probably the lad had made himself hungry. He would be down in the refectory gobbling the last muffin.

How serious was his drug problem? Was the boy an addict? Curiously, Father Bingley had never confronted drug addiction directly in his pastoral work. He understood that the parish of St. Dinarius was not without its substance abusers, but he himself had never dealt with them as such. What usually happened was that a son or daughter of the parish stopped coming to church, first of all, and then disappeared from the community entirely. Sometimes he discovered (Martha would tell him) that the young person was in rehab or had run away to the city. Once in a while there was an overdose or a car crash and he had to bury the child.

Thanks be to God these incidents had slacked off greatly in the last ten years, perhaps because the parishioners were aging. A matter of demographics. The younger priests had been trained at seminary in how to deal with alcoholism and drug addiction, but when Father Bingley went to school, such things were not a consideration.

And yet. Was he missing an opportunity to do the Lord's work? A mark against him, when the time came to render up his accounting.

He resolved to save Jonathan Newmont if he could. The straying sheep might be down in the refectory even now. If Father Bingley found him there, he would speak to him; if not, he would at least avail himself of one of Brother Mortimer's muffins, or a ripe banana, or a handful of sweet grapes, and have words with the boy tomorrow.

Wall sconces cast a faint yellow-orange glow to illuminate the hallway for late-arriving travelers, but the route through the library to the refectory was not lighted. Father Bingley's stomach rumbled. He groped along, thinking of fruit.

Feeding the flesh. Next week he would think more deeply about the things the doctor had said to him, warnings about the condition of his arteries, about his sugar. He might be a tad overweight, but he was as vigorous as he had ever been, still in the prime of life, scarcely more than sixty. Surely his best work lay before him. Furthermore he felt fine, easy and comfortable in his body, the aches and pains of old age far away. It was good to taste food, good to fill his belly.

Then suddenly he saw it, a figure in black robes, sitting silently in the corner of the library, waiting, perhaps for him. The Angel of Death.

Not yet! No! There's so much more to do! Without meaning to, Father Bingley made a sound—"ulp," or "yip"—and staggered backward, his hair all on end. The figure raised its hooded head and seemed to look at him accusingly.

It had no face.

Next morning at matins Brother Basil's quavering voice was missing from the chant, and Mother Grey feared that he must be ill. At breakfast his pale face was still nowhere to be seen. A feverish state of agitation seemed to animate the other monks, as much as could be expressed in perfect silence. One of them dropped his coffee. When Mortimer appeared with his broom a moment later, he was not smiling.

In silence Mother Grey savored her granola with strawberries and sunflower seeds and considered the nocturnal noises. Were they typical of a night in the monastery guesthouse? It seemed so unlikely. Had Deedee heard them?

She was dying to gossip about it, but to speak now was against the rules.

After breakfast she returned to the library, bent on mortifying her worldly urge to natter. Something was wrong, she knew it; so many anguished glances flew from eye to eye.

When the Great Silence was lifted at last, she got up and crossed the room for a chatfest with Deedee. But it was not to be. Brother Fergus suddenly appeared in the library. He gathered all the guests together and herded them into the corner, where Delight van Buskirk sat counting the stitches in a tiny bit of lace. From Deedee's anxious face Mother Grey gathered that this was not the standard procedure for a Sunday morning.

Quite a few people were gathered in the herd, including all of Bingley's flock and most of the youth group from California.

"I have some disturbing news," Brother Fergus said. "Our Brother Basil disappeared last night. I was hoping one of you might remember seeing or hearing something that would help us find him."

Exclamations of surprise and alarm. Mother Grey reviewed in her mind the thumps and rustlings of the night before, considering whether anything she had heard might help in locating Basil.

"Black monks," said Delight van Buskirk, pausing in her work.

"Black monks?" Martine marveled.

"Well, no," the old lady said, "the monks weren't black, or at least I couldn't tell whether they were black or not, you know how the hoods hang over their faces. Their habits were some dark color. It seemed to be black in the night."

"Our habits are all white," Brother Fergus said, "except

for the novice's habit. Are you sure it was more than one monk?"

"Maybe I dreamed it," said the old lady.

"What were the black monks doing?" Deedee said.

"I thought I heard a sound. I got up and looked outside."

"Through the window of your room?" Mother Grey said.

"Through the window of St. Dymphna, the bathroom window. I looked outside, and there they were, two monks dressed all in black, carrying Our Lord across the lawn on his heavenly throne."

"Indeed," Fergus said, passing his hand over his thick gray curls.

"That's what I saw." Delight van Buskirk frowned and began to count stitches again, muttering numbers under her breath. When she came to the end of the row, she said, "Do you think I might have been dreaming?"

"I expect so." He looked around at the rest of the group. "Did anyone else see anything?"

Ouida Sedgewick cleared her throat. Everyone stared at her, but she said nothing, though her face spoke volumes of rage and turmoil.

"Mrs. Sedgewick?"

"I'd rather not say."

"Speak up, lady," said Deedee. "If it has anything to do with Brother Basil's disappearance, the sooner we hear it the better."

She drew in a breath and let it out sharply. "I saw a monk in the guest quarters last night."

"In black robes?"

"No, no, white robes, just like yours. He was—oh—"

"He was what?"

"Going into one of the guest rooms."

"In the night?"

"Sometime shortly after midnight, I think. I heard a

sound in the hall, and I put my head out the door, just to see what it was."

Brother Fergus rubbed the back of his neck. "We're all long in our beds by midnight."

"This one was in somebody else's bed."

"A monk?" said Deedee. "Surely you're not suggesting that Brother Basil—"

"Is that what that noise was!" said Mrs. Bingley. "Didn't I tell you, Rupert, that I thought I heard bedsprings bouncing?" They all looked at her. She blushed, accused out of her own mouth of talking during the Great Silence.

Nobody said anything. Deedee caught Mother Grey's eye, and the two of them had to struggle to keep their faces straight. The mere idea of the elderly Brother Basil creeping about the guest quarters after hours, with lustful intent! It was too silly.

"Did you see where the monk went, Mrs. Sedgewick?" Fergus asked. "Which guest room?"

"It was—"

"Oh, squat," Delight van Buskirk muttered.

"Is something wrong, Mrs. van Buskirk?"

"I've lost one of my knitting needles," she said. "It's a nice old steel double-O. You can hardly find them these days." She held up the mate to the missing needle, long, narrow, pointed, and gleaming, with a bit of knitted lace hanging off it. "Ever since I had my cataracts removed, I've been able to do this fine work again," she said. "But I don't know where to find steel needles anymore."

For no particular reason except that she had fallen asleep the night before reading a whodunit, the sight of the knitting needle gave Mother Grey the shivers. "Where could it have gone?"

"Nowhere. I left my knitting bag hanging right here on

this chair all night long." She stuffed the work back into the bag with a sigh of annoyance.

"Down the hall and to the right from our room," Ouida said. "When I looked out I had an impression of a large white figure, and a woman's hand darting out and pulling him inside."

"I myself went downstairs in the night," said Father Bingley. "It could have been after midnight. I thought I saw someone."

"Basil?" Fergus said.

"No. I thought I saw another monk, all dressed in black robes. He was sitting over there, in the dark." The memory of it seemed to make him uncomfortable, fearful even. Mother Grey thought of the black-clad figure she had seen before matins on Saturday. Menacing? Hardly. Oh, well, maybe if you met him in the dark.

"You saw someone in black robes in the guesthouse?" Fergus said.

"Startled me, actually," said Bingley. "I was hungry in the night. I got up for a piece of fruit."

Fergus rubbed his hair some more.

Deedee, with a notebook and pencil, was trying to write everything down. "That was after midnight, you say. And what time did you see the monk in white, Mrs. Sedgewick?" she asked.

"I guess it was after midnight. I'm not sure."

"Perhaps your husband looked at a clock."

"I'm afraid he wasn't—"

"I was in the bathroom at the time," Rodman Sedgewick said. "I woke up with a headache, and I got up to take something for it. Nothing unusual was going on, as far as I could see."

"What time was that?" Deedee asked.

"Ten after twelve."

Deedee made a notation in her book.

"Did you see anyone else while you were up?" asked Fergus.

"No. No one."

Berry Newmont piped up. "I find sometimes that it's difficult to sleep when you're expecting to get up very early the next morning. Don't you find that?" She tossed her yellow curls over her shoulder, almost a nervous mannerism. Ouida Sedgewick looked daggers at her.

"And so?" Mother Grey said.

"Excuse me?"

"Did you have trouble sleeping last night?"

"No. No trouble. As a matter of fact I slept very well. But sometimes it's hard, is what I'm saying."

"Oh, yes," Delight van Buskirk suddenly exclaimed. "There was one other thing. Before the Lord on his throne, I saw the ghosts."

"What ghosts?" asked Fergus.

"The ghosts of two monks, one white and one black. They were carrying a coffin down the back stairs."

My word. Mother Grey resolved to have a talk with the old dear's granddaughter. She probably shouldn't be living alone.

"I can tell you the exact time of that," the old lady said. "I checked the time just before I got up to go to the bathroom." She looked around at their faces and saw embarrassment and pity reflected back. "I suppose now you're going to tell me this monastery isn't haunted."

"Not that we're aware of," said Brother Fergus gently. "Some of the medieval monasteries in Europe are said to be haunted, but St. Hugh's is only about a hundred years old. Nothing very terrible has ever gone on here." He looked around himself apprehensively. "That we know of."

"What time was it, then?" Deedee asked. "When you saw the ghosts."

"It was a little after twelve."

"Thanks." Deedee wrote it down. "Anybody else?"

The children of the youth group were all outside in their tents the whole night long, they said. The field where they camped was down by the river, on the other side of a thick woodlot. They had seen and heard nothing.

Martine had gotten up in the night also, she said. When she first put her head out of her room, she had received the impression of a monk going down the dim hall toward the Sedgewicks' quarters, dressed in white robes. She wasn't sure of the time.

Nobody could say for certain, with all the hubbub, that they either had or hadn't seen the elderly monk. The Smartts weren't in the crowd, Mother Grey noted. Out running, Martine said.

"I can talk to them later, if need be," Fergus said. "Thank you all for your help." Most of the grownups left the gathering and fled upstairs. The young folks began gathering their backpacks.

"What do you think?" said Deedee.

"I don't know," Fergus said. "Basil is not a young man anymore. We thought he was in good health, but it's possible that he wandered into the guesthouse and had some sort of attack."

"Let's go look for him," said Deedee.

Fergus rubbed his hair again. "It's almost time for Holy Eucharist."

One of the teenagers volunteered to help in the search; Fergus was pleased to accept the offer and drafted two more of them.

"Right. You, you, and you"—he pointed to three strapping fellows—"you be my search party. Go upstairs and search the guesthouse for Brother Basil. Check—I don't know, check the floor of the linen closet, under the beds, anyplace an old man might have had some sort of attack and passed out. Come to me at once if you find him; I'll be in the chapel."

5

Mother Grey went upstairs too. As she looked down the hall toward her room, she saw a figure in white going into the men's bathroom.

"Basil!" she called, but he didn't look around.

Roger Smartt and his wife came up the stairs behind her, puffing and perspiring, their running shoes tracking mud.

"Brother Basil is missing," she told them. "I think I may have seen him go into the men's bathroom just now. Roger, could you go in there and see if it's him?"

"What would Basil be doing in the guesthouse bathroom?" Annabelle said. Mother Grey shrugged.

Roger Smartt came out again. "There's no one in there except Rodman Sedgewick," he said.

"My word. How could I have mistaken Sedgewick for Basil?" They were nothing alike.

"He's wearing a white bathrobe; it looks almost like a monk's habit. He says he's planning to take a shower."

"Ah," she said. Maybe from the back, stooping over in his floppy robe, Sedgewick at a great distance and without one's glasses could pass for Basil. It must have been the clothing.

And then the bell rang for the next service.

People from the nearby towns came to the Sunday Eucharist, whole families who seemed to use St. Hugh's as their parish church. A little boy of three or so ran up to receive, laughing, his hands stretched out one on top of the other. The sight of him charmed Mother Grey completely. It was an image that was to stay with her long after the unpleasantness was all but forgotten.

"Let's go and take a look at the river," Father Bingley's wife said to him after Eucharist.

"Not now," he said. "There's something I want to do first." He had it in his mind to return to the spot where he had frightened himself last night. Martha had pointed out to him that he had eaten very little breakfast. Probably better so, if he wished to preserve his mortal life for many more years. Still, it was the sign of a troubled soul. He needed comfort. He wanted to see whether there might not be some earthly explanation for the appearance of the Death Angel as he went last night to get a snack.

"I'm going for a walk by myself, then," Martha said. "I need the exercise. We'll meet at diurnum."

No one was in the library. The morning sun came slanting through the windows, lighting all the shadows and dark places. A reading lamp cast a cheerful yellow circle in the corner where Death had seemed to be sitting. Clearly there was no one there now. As an experiment, he took a step backward, posing himself where he had been standing when he saw the thing, hoping to surprise some sort of optical illusion. Nothing changed; the chair was empty still.

What had it been? An omen? A creature of his imagination? One of Mrs. van Buskirk's ghosts?

He approached the spot. This would have been where the apparition was sitting, this odd little armchair. Nothing about it now seemed menacing. It was merely quaint; the curious design on the back, the rush seat, the queer legs with rails around three sides of the bottom instead of halfway up the legs where rungs would normally go. A simple oak footstool covered in dark leather was placed invitingly in front of the armchair. He considered sitting down to think until he noticed that one of the legs of the footstool was resting in a stain, a darker red on the dark red tiles, soaked into the grout, sticky, and about as big around as a big Communion wafer.

Death, he thought. He went to tell Brother Fergus about the stain.

In response to Fergus's call, two of the local police came over the winding mountain road, patrolmen Timmerman and Case from Vandervliet-on-Hudson. Mother Grey saw them arrive; Fergus received them in the library. Handsome fellows in uniform. *How young they look*, Mother Grey thought. *They say that's the first sign of middle age, when all the policemen start to look young to you.*

Fergus explained the situation to them as best he could. They seemed uncomfortable in a monastery. Mother Grey wondered fleetingly whether either of them attended church. They asked a few questions, took a few statements, looked at the stain and then at each other.

"What makes you think Brother Basil might be a victim

of foul play?" Timmerman asked the prior. "Don't you think maybe he just took off?"

Plainly written in the glances they exchanged was the fact that either Timmerman or Case would have fled the monastery a long time ago, in Basil's place. Poverty? Chastity? Obedience? Why would anyone stick around here and suffer the life of a monk?

"It's very unlikely that he left of his own will," Fergus said. "Basil is eighty-five years old. Quite apart from the fact that he is committed to living here—this is his home— he knows he could never walk out over the mountain. Certainly not at night."

"Unless he had some kind of spell," Case said. "Lost his memory and wandered away. Old guys do that sometimes."

"And the bloodstain?"

"Bumped his nose," Timmerman offered. "Or bumped his head, lost his memory. Don't suppose you checked the doors this morning to see if any of them were unlocked."

"The guesthouse is never kept locked. But you know, if Basil is out wandering, he's in danger of succumbing to exposure. It's cold out and still wet from last night's storm."

"Tell you what," Timmerman offered. "We'll call in a helicopter, help you look for him. Eighty-five—I guess, as you say, he can't have gotten very far. You keep looking. We'll be back with more help in an hour or so."

They went away again, leaving Fergus to retire to his office in great consternation, still certain that something terrible had happened. The other monks went back outside to search the rainy weeds for some trace of Basil. All except for Mortimer. He suddenly appeared with his mop, and before Mother Grey could utter the words "crime scene," he had cleaned up the bloodstain and gone away again.

Deedee plopped herself into the morris chair that Mother Grey thought of as hers and shuffled through her list of nocturnal monk-sightings, chewing her pencil. Mother Grey looked around, shrugged, sat down beside her, and put her feet up on the fatal footstool. *What the hell,* she thought. Not even the police thought the scene was worth preserving.

"So what do you think, Deedee?" she said. "Is Basil's disappearance the work of ghostly monks?"

"The only ghosts I'd expect to find in here are the spirits of Gustave Stickley and the Roycrofters."

"What's that? A fifties rock band?"

"Famous designers of mission furniture. Surely you've heard of them, the Roycrofters; Gustave Stickley, Frank Lloyd Wright. . . . No, the clue here is novice robes," Deedee said.

"What about them?"

"Whatever is going on, that novice is probably behind it. He's the one in the black robe."

"Should we try to talk to him?"

"Certainly."

"Where is he, then? In the monks' quarters?"

"Fergus will know."

She went with Deedee to find Fergus, through a heavy oak door and into the hall behind the chapel. Halfway down this hall was the door to the prior's office. At the end of the hall was another door bearing the carved sign, "Cloistered—Guests Please Keep Out."

As they stepped into the hallway, Mother Grey heard a distant whine. She thought for an instant that it was some sort of alarm—women approaching the monks' quarters!— but when the door closed behind them, the sound grew clearer, and she recognized it as the snarl of power woodworking tools. Octavian or one of the others at work on the honest furniture. Work was an important part of the Benedictine rule.

Fergus was at his desk, stewing. He looked up and greeted them.

"We were hoping we could be of some help," Mother Grey said.

"We've decided that the mystery will be solved when we find two black novice robes," Deedee said. *We have?* It sounded a little simplistic to Mother Grey, if not downright simpleminded; nevertheless she allowed herself to be included in Deedee's "we." Sometimes her friend had a way of cutting through to the essentials by abandoning any pretense at logic.

"Novice robes. Brother Christophe is the only novice at St. Hugh's right now," said Fergus. "But he does have two black habits. Sometimes one is in the wash, you know."

"Ah," said Mother Grey. The thing began to take shape. Someone he knew out in the world could have sneaked into the monastery and borrowed Christophe's spare habit for camouflage. Then the two of them . . .

"Why doesn't Christophe come to meals?" Deedee said.

"Christophe is going through a hard time right now. He keeps to himself."

"May we talk to him?" Mother Grey asked.

"Why?"

"We won't bite him or anything, Fergus," Deedee said. "We just want to—"

"Interrogate him?"

"Hardly. It's just that all this talk about dark monks . . ."

"He's outside working." Brother Fergus pulled aside the window drapery to reveal the monastery's herb garden. So! They did have one! It was shaped like a wheel, looking extremely scraggly and sad, no doubt due to the late freeze. Christophe crouched over it, weeding, his hood up over his head, his thin narrow back turned toward them. The hand that troweled bits of green from the muddy earth was as black as his habit.

"He's African American!" cried Deedee, striving to hit the currently correct term.

"Well, no, actually, he's simply African. I'll introduce you. Please, please don't say anything to upset him. He's terribly sensitive."

They went into the walled garden, which was part of the cloistered monks' quarters, not usually accessible to guests. Christophe looked up at the sound of their footsteps. His face was unlined, expressionless, deep, deep black. Mother Grey would have called him a boy. You could tell he was— damaged? a foreigner? the victim of some atrocity?—from his lack of animation. A growing heap of murdered hardy perennials lay beside his industrious elbow.

"Mother Grey, Deacon Gilchrist, this is Christophe," said Fergus.

"How do you do," said Mother Grey.

"How do you do." Christophe's voice was soft and heavily accented.

"I think that's thyme, dear," said Deedee. "You want to let it grow."

"Not a weed?"

"No."

"Sorry." He tried to stick the little roots back in the hole. It might work.

"Your English is very good. How long have you been in this country?" Mother Grey said.

Dropping his trowel, Christophe turned his face to Fergus with a wild beseeching look.

"Mother Grey and Deacon Gilchrist want to ask you about your clothing," said Fergus, stepping around questions of immigration. "They thought someone might have come into your quarters in the night and borrowed your habit."

"I don't think so," said Christophe. "I would have heard them. I sleep very lightly."

"Did you get up last night, Christophe?" Deedee said.

"Up?"

"Were you in the guesthouse?" Mother Grey said.

"Only to help Brother Basil with the chest."

"What chest?" Fergus said.

"Basil wanted to put his chest in the guesthouse. I helped him carry it down the stairs. It's heavy, even without—even when it's empty."

"In the night?" Fergus said. "You carried it past my room, and I heard nothing?"

"We took it down the guesthouse stairs. We didn't speak," said Christophe. "Carrying things during the Great Silence is not forbidden, is it?"

Ah. The coffin. "Can you show us this chest?" Mother Grey said.

"You want me to go into the guesthouse?"

"If you will, please."

He put his hood up over his face and folded his hands in his sleeves.

Mother Grey hadn't noticed Basil's chest before Christophe showed it to them, pushed up against the wall behind two chairs and a table, where you would never see it unless you went looking.

"Not old," Deedee said. "Maybe fifty. Not stylish either." It was simple and plain, made of roughly finished teakwood, not even fumed oak.

But it was large. A good place to look for a body; maybe even two.

Fergus lifted the lid. Mother Grey held her breath.

Except for the key lying on the bottom, the chest was

empty. Of course, if Basil had been carrying it, he could hardly have been in it, could he?

"Smells like the Orient," Deedee said.

"The Orient?" Fergus said.

"China. I had a friend who came back from China with a chest like that, and it had this smell. Teakwood. Or Chinese mushrooms. Something." It also smelled like a body, Mother Grey thought. Not a dead body—a live body, as in body odor.

"Basil is quite a traveler," said Fergus. "I expect this chest has been all over the world."

The odd thing was the holes. Normally you wouldn't bore holes in a chest you expected to keep woolens or foodstuffs in, for fear of insects. Maybe he slept in it, some sort of monastic penance.

Fergus lowered the lid again. "Did Brother Basil tell you why he wanted this put in the guesthouse, Christophe?"

"No, Father. He wanted to make some space, was all he said."

"Hm. His room is rather small. Perhaps he means to take up yoga and needs the floor space."

"At eighty-five years of age?" Deedee said.

"He's been playing cards with the Zen monks at the ashram up the road," Fergus said. "They give him all sorts of ideas."

"What did he do with the things that were in the chest?" Mother Grey said.

"There was nothing in the chest," said Christophe.

"We don't have a lot of possessions," Fergus explained.

"But when Basil came here, what did he bring with him in this chest?"

Again Christophe gave Fergus the wild look. Again he seemed poised for flight. But before the little dark novice could take off, Brother Octavian came running in. His boating mocs smacked on the tile floor; his white habit bellied out behind him.

"We found Basil, Father. He was lying in the bushes next to the garden wall." Fergus stared at him, waiting to hear the worst. "I'm afraid he's dead. He seems to have been— there's a knitting needle sticking out of his back."

So. What this retreat was about, after all, was murder.

6

"I can't imagine who would do such a thing," said Fergus. Mother Grey and Deedee shuffled fretfully around the office, trying to think of something to do, while Fergus dialed the police.

"Maybe it was someone who wanted to keep him quiet," Deedee ventured. "Did he know any secrets?"

"Brother Basil was spiritual adviser to many people. No doubt they told him things—hello?"

Some monk with a bad conscience? Would one of these men murder a fellow monk? *Surely not.*

The emergency people came on the line, and Fergus reported to them the finding of Basil's body. A folder labeled LIBERIA rested on Fergus's desk. Mother Grey flipped it open idly, but the photograph that met her eyes was so distressing that she immediately closed it again. Atrocity pictures.

Fergus hung up the phone. "In half an hour," he said, "the full might of the county of Ulster will descend on St. Hugh's."

"Good," Deedee said. "They'll clear up everything."

"Yes, whether we want them to or not," Fergus said, exhibiting increased agitation.

"Fergus! Are you hiding something here?"

"Let's just say that there are elements at St. Hugh's that we'd just as soon not expose to the light of official scrutiny," he said.

"You're hiding Brother Christophe," Mother Grey said.

"The immigration authorities are unaware of his presence among us," Fergus said. "We'd like to keep it that way."

"What's his story?" Mother Grey asked.

"He's a Liberian orphan, the last survivor of a village wiped out by a tribal death squad. His parents were hacked to pieces before his eyes."

"The poor kid," Deedee said.

"He was drafted into the army at the age of fourteen," Fergus continued.

"By which faction?"

"The same people who murdered everyone in his village. Eventually he was able to desert."

"So what's he doing here?" Deedee asked. "In a monastery? Does he have a vocation to be a religious, or—"

"We're simply hiding him."

"You mean he isn't a real postulant?" Deedee said.

"He says he wants to join us, but he's only seventeen, and we like our postulants to have some experience of the world, preferably some college education, before they make a lifetime commitment to a cloistered life."

"What will he do if he doesn't become a monk?" Mother Grey asked.

"Time will tell, I suppose. He's been helping Mortimer in the kitchen, and Octavian in the workshop. Food service and carpentry are good careers. We plan to help him make a life in the world if he isn't called to stay with us."

"Hiding him from the federal authorities," Mother Grey said. "An illegal alien."

"Yes," said Fergus, "certainly. There is no more important concept in the Judeo-Christian tradition than the way we treat aliens. Had Christophe stayed in Liberia, he would almost certainly have been killed. He will almost certainly be killed if he goes back there. The situation is very bad. I have pictures, if you want to see them. Whole villages, decapitated or worse—"

"That's okay," Deedee said.

"We understand," said Mother Grey. She had seen enough when she opened the folder.

"If the immigration authorities find Christophe, they'll send him back, after holding him in one of their jails for a year or two. As I said, he's only a boy. Basil believed, and I agreed, that we should keep him with us until our prayers and petitions were answered for a change in the immigration laws."

"We're all praying for an improvement to the immigration laws," said Mother Grey. "Our treatment of refugees, especially people of color, has been so heartless—"

"I meant petitions to Congress," said Fergus. "The Church has a lobbying arm in Washington that's sometimes quite effective. Campaign funds are always in short supply for our lawmakers. We do what we can."

So the monks were lining up to buy lawmakers? And people thought these folks were unworldly. "How did Basil get Christophe into the country?" Mother Grey asked.

"You know that chest in the library, the one with the holes?"

"My word."

"Even hidden in that chest," Deedee said, "how could he—"

"They came by boat. Basil brought him over in that chest through the port of Halifax, then overland by car. It's almost impossible to get anyone into this country illegally by air. The immigration authorities would have arrested him at once and taken him straight to the Pike County Jail in Hawley, Pennsylvania, held him for a couple of years, and then—"

"Why Pike County?"

"That's where they're holding many of the East Coast illegal aliens these days. The immigration service rents jail space."

So Basil had smuggled him in. Such a brave, sweet old man. And now he had been killed. Why? What had there been in Basil's life that would prompt someone to murder him?

And why did he want the chest out of his room? The motives of monks. Perhaps he kept some sort of record of his thoughts.

"Do you think you can continue to hide Christophe after the police get here?" Deedee said. "Surely they'll want to look into everything, examine everybody."

"That's what I was thinking," said Fergus. "If only we could give them the solution when they arrive, then perhaps—"

"Great," Deedee said. "Then we have half an hour to do our stuff."

"What stuff?" Mother Grey said.

"Our detective stuff."

"If you can solve this crime in half an hour," Fergus said, "you may be able to save my novice from the immigration authorities."

Look for motives, Mother Grey thought. "Did Basil keep a journal?" she asked.

"You mean a diary?" Fergus said.

"Anything that would shed light on the unknown parts of his life."

"I'll go look around his room and see."

"We should talk to Martine, also," Deedee said.

"Who is Martine?" Fergus said.

"Martine Wellworth, the young black woman we brought with us from St. Bede's," said Mother Grey. "She's a criminal lawyer."

"She'll have a viewpoint," said Deedee. "Doubtless."

"But what if it turns out that Christophe is the murderer?" Mother Grey said.

Fergus shook his head. "Christophe would never have harmed Basil. He loved him. Basil saved his life many, many times."

They found Martine in her room, St. Francis of Assisi, sitting on the narrow bed looking miserable. Mother Grey hoped she wasn't still angry at her.

"Martine," she said, "we need you. We have half an hour to find a killer."

"Twenty-five minutes, actually," said Deedee, looking at her watch. "So let's get busy."

Martine stared at them.

"I'm sorry about the fight we had," said Mother Grey. "Forget everything I said."

"Oh, that," Martine said. "I'm sorry too, Vinnie. Forget what I said too. All I can say is, I'm not myself right now. I've been under a strain."

"Because you're being passed over for partner at Sneckman, Flammis, Flammis, and Wray?"

"It isn't that. It's Albert. Rodman Sedgewick let him go last week."

"What!"

"He trumped up some pretext, saying he'd offended an important client by something he did, but it was just to cover himself so that Albert wouldn't bring an action against the firm. It's all part of a pattern of racism."

"Are you all right? Is Albert okay?"

"He's talking about pulling up stakes and going back to the Bahamas. Meanwhile I'm pregnant again."

"Oh, my dear." Mother Grey took her in her arms and patted her on the back. Her shoulders felt thin as a bird's. "You should have said something."

"I did, but it wasn't what I meant to say. This is kind of difficult to deal with." She sat up straight and pulled herself together with a visible effort. "What's all this about finding a killer?"

"Brother Basil is dead," said Mother Grey. "They found him with a knitting needle in his back."

"Oh, no! I hope they don't think—"

"I'm sure no one thinks Delight did it. You know how she leaves her knitting lying around. The problem is that we have to protect the novice." In as few words as possible, they told her all about Christophe, how he was in danger of being discovered, deported, and killed.

"So in"—Martine looked at her watch—"twenty minutes, you want me to help you pin the crime on someone else."

"Yes, yes," said Deedee.

"Who, for instance?"

Mother Grey considered Bingley, briefly, then rejected the idea as being too personally convenient. Anyway, he had no motive that she could think of. "I like Rodman Sedgewick for it," she said.

"Any particular reason?" Martine said. "Aside from the fact that we'd all like to see him behind bars, I mean."

"And the fact that he once tried to kill you," Deedee said.

"Allegedly," Martine said.

How to make a case out of her gut feeling about Rodman Sedgewick? "There's something suspicious about the man," Mother Grey said.

"Oh, I agree. Rodman Sedgewick is a cad and a bounder," Martine said.

"A pimple on the bee-hind of the body politic," Deedee said. "But still—"

"How can this fact help us to save the life of the illegal Liberian immigrant that Fergus is hiding in the monks' quarters, disguised as a novice?" Martine said. "In twenty minutes or less, I might add."

"There's some odd story about Rodman Sedgewick's mother," Mother Grey said lamely.

A shadow moved across the glass.

Mother Grey opened the door, and there stood Rodman Sedgewick himself.

"I thought I heard my name," he said.

"I don't think so," said Mother Grey.

"Is it true that Fergus is hiding an illegal immigrant?"

"That's something you'll have to take up with Fergus. His affairs are his own."

"My affairs are my own also," said Rodman Sedgewick. "If you ladies want to pry into them, it could turn out to be very unpleasant. I hope I've made myself clear." He turned on his heel and went away. Mother Grey watched him all the way down the hall.

"Was he threatening us?" Deedee asked.

"He was threatening us," Martine said.

"But with what?"

"Unpleasantness," Mother Grey said.

"No fear. He's unpleasant already," Deedee said.

"Let him do his worst, then," Martine said. "How much do you think he heard?"

"Not much, I hope." Mother Grey closed the door and lowered her voice. "But listen. Basil knew something about him. Remember that business with the cups, Deedee? Sedgewick broke all those mugs on purpose so Basil wouldn't keep saying what he was saying."

"And what was he saying?" said Martine softly.

"Something about Sedgewick when he was in prep school in Switzerland," Deedee murmured. They were all speaking in low voices. Sedgewick had ears like a bat; if he wasn't in the hall, he could be in either of the adjoining rooms with a water tumbler pressed against the wall.

"Maybe he cheated on his exams," said Mother Grey.

"That was an awfully long time ago, Vinnie. Rodman Sedgewick is—dear me!—ten or fifteen years older than I am. What could he have done in prep school that would be worth killing somebody to hush up after all these years? Especially after the things you did to trash his reputation."

"It wasn't exactly Sedgewick's reputation that I trashed. The reason his political career is ruined is that he can't run for high office without attracting media attention to his relatives."

"He's still a prominent man," Martine said. "I'd say he has plenty to lose."

"Yes," Deedee said. "His right-wing cronies could turn against him, or his jealous wife. The money is all hers, right?"

"So they say. But what could have happened thirty years ago that would bother his wife today?"

Martine shrugged. "He was gay?"

"He killed somebody? He fathered a child?" Mother Grey said.

"He got it on with his horses?" Deedee said.

Mother Grey said, "It's something about his late mother."

"Go ask Delight van Buskirk," Martine said. "She's been around forever. Maybe she's heard something."

"If she knew what his secret was, he would have whacked her a long time ago," Deedee said. "If he's into whacking people."

"Unless Sedgewick was counting on nobody believing her," Mother Grey said. "She's getting a little . . ."

"Go ask her anyhow," Martine said. "I'll try to think of some other ways to proceed. Though frankly, I don't think we're going to be able to accomplish much in"—she looked at her watch again—"ten minutes."

As the news of Basil's death spread, the atmosphere of the monastery chilled considerably. Looking back on it later, Mother Grey thought she remembered seeing monks standing here and there in the hallways in attitudes of grief, like funerary sculptures, but that couldn't have been. Monks are busy people, and when one of their number goes to his reward, they miss him, but they carry on. Perhaps she caught one of them weeping in the hall, or two.

In the library the guests had dropped their voices to the lowest murmur, out of respect for the gravity of the situation. Annabelle Smartt sat in the middle of an old oak settle, quietly holding court, showing a lot of leg, surrounded by breathless boys from the youth group. Young Jonathan Newmont was getting the whole scene on videotape.

"Yes, my dears, a diary," she was saying. "Brother Basil told all."

Now, how did she hear about that? thought Mother Grey.

"Told all about what?" Jonathan Newmont said. "An old monk."

"The story of lust in his heart for young postulants or visiting women."

"Yeah, right."

"Maybe he made a pass at someone who stabbed him to death in outrage," she suggested. As she and Deedee squeezed past the back of the settle, Mother Grey found herself wondering whether it would be worthwhile to consume any of their remaining ten minutes trying to shut this rowdy woman up.

"So, tell us," said one of the bolder boys. "Did he put the moves on you?"

"Well, my dear—" Annabelle Smartt suddenly made a noise like "awk" or "ulp" and fell silent. Mother Grey glanced over her shoulder to see Deedee smirking, and Annabelle excusing herself and leaving the room.

"What did you do, hit her?"

"Hit her? No. I snapped her behind the ear."

"What do you mean?"

"You take your middle finger and thumb and go *snap!* It's a sure way to bring someone to his senses. My Irish grandmother used to do it to me all the time. She learned it from a nun."

"These days they call that sort of thing abuse, Deedee. Or assault, if you're doing it to a grownup."

"Did the job, though, didn't it?" said Deedee.

They found Delight van Buskirk sitting in Mother Grey's morris chair, struggling to read a book with the aid of a magnifying glass.

"You look unnatural without your knitting," Mother Grey said.

The old lady sighed. "I feel unnatural. I don't see why they can't let me have it back. Or, yes, I do see, but just the same I wish they'd give it to me."

"Your knitting needle," said Mother Grey.

"Can't knit with just one needle."

"Mrs. van Buskirk!" Deedee said, plunging in. "What do you know about Rodman Sedgewick's past?"

The old lady closed her book and put the magnifying glass in her knitting bag. "Not much at all, dear."

"Ah. Too bad."

"Why do you ask?"

"We think Brother Basil might have known something about him that he wanted to keep quiet," Mother Grey said. "Something that happened when he was in school."

"Roddy Sedgewick was all grown up by the time his family moved to Bountiful Horse Farms," Mrs. van Buskirk said. "Grown and gone off to college."

"When was that?"

"It's hard to remember. The year Eisenhower was first elected president, I think it was. Wade Sedgewick came from Washington to settle down with his new bride."

"Was he a Democrat, then?" Rodman Sedgewick's father, a Democrat! The idea boggled the mind.

"No, no. But he wasn't an Eisenhower man. And then his wife had a baby. That was Ellen. You remember her, dear. She came to our church for a while."

"So Rodman was the child of Wade Sedgewick's first marriage," Deedee said.

"Yes," Mrs. van Buskirk said. "Or so they said. The first wife died."

"Rodman's mother."

"Yes."

"What was she like?"

"We never knew. She was dead, you see."

"Well, then, thanks anyhow."

"You're welcome."

As she spoke, they realized that their free half hour had fled away. The first wave of law enforcement officers burst into the library in the shape of patrolmen Timmerman and Case, followed closely by a plainclothes officer, who seemed to be in charge, and a crowd of his minions.

As everyone else in the library sat frozen in watchful attitudes, Rodman Sedgewick sprang from his seat and approached the plainclothes officer, hand extended. "I'm Rodman Sedgewick," he said. "My wife and I are staying here this weekend."

"Detective Francis X. O'Rourke," said the officer, shaking his hand.

"As you know, there's been a murder here," Sedgewick said. "I've done some soul-searching and I've decided to tell you what happened, regardless of the consequences."

Mother Grey's heart leaped. *He's going to confess!*

7

Father Bingley rose to his feet. What was this? What did Rodman Sedgewick know about the old monk's murder? Surely Sedgewick wasn't about to say he had committed it himself. Someone should go and fetch Fergus. But here he was now, white robes flying, arriving just in time to hear Sedgewick's announcement.

"The monks are hiding an illegal alien in their quarters," Sedgewick trumpeted. "They have him disguised as a novice."

Everyone turned to look at Sedgewick, and then at Fergus, expecting him to deny it.

"A Liberian," Sedgewick continued. "Clearly this person murdered Brother Basil to keep him from turning him in to the federal immigration authorities."

"A librarian?" the plainclothes officer said, scratching in his notebook.

"A Liberian. From Africa," Sedgewick amplified. Fergus said nothing. If he wasn't denying the story, it must be so. Father Bingley had heard of the political activism of certain monks, but this was taking things a bit far. Actually it sounded like the sort of stunt Lavinia Grey would get up to, concealing illegals in the sanctuary.

"Is what he says true?" the detective asked Brother Fergus.

"It's true that we have a visitor from Liberia in the monks' quarters," Fergus said. "Mr. Sedgewick is mistaken in his other assertions."

"Just the same," the detective said, "I'd like to see this person." When Fergus expressed reluctance, he said, "We can get a warrant."

"If you'll wait here, I can go and get him," Fergus said.

"If you don't mind, I'd like him to have a police escort," O'Rourke said. "Timmerman, Case, go with the holy father here." The prior and the two policemen made their way into the back hall, heading for the monks' quarters.

Father Bingley resumed his seat. Martha seemed anxious. He patted her hand. "We'll leave for home soon," he told her. "Another hour, I should think."

It was Brother Octavian who offered to take the rest of the detective's entourage outside and show them the place where Basil's body was lying. Everyone else seemed to have forgotten the poor old fellow in all this brouhaha about aliens. Father Bingley said a silent prayer for the slain monk's soul, and when he looked up again, Rodman Sedgewick was putting his arm around the shoulder of the detective.

It was almost as though Sedgewick were campaigning for office again. Father Bingley hadn't seen him quite so hail-fellow-well-met and just-between-us in his manner since that Sunday morning when he brought the governor with him to St. Dinarius. Why was he troubling to butter up this police detective? Looking for another vote for his flat tax? But no, it appeared that he had some theory to expound concerning the murder. Indeed he was hot at it, with the other arm, the arm not around the detective's shoulder, sawing the air emphatically.

"No other plausible explanation," he was saying. "I'm sure you'll agree."

"What makes you think so?" the detective asked.

"Motive. Poor Brother Basil must have threatened to turn him in to the immigration authorities," Sedgewick said.

"I still don't understand why he would do that."

"Don't you? It seems clear to me. For one thing, it was no more than Basil's duty as a concerned citizen. So this ignorant savage, from Togo or wherever it was—"

"You mentioned Liberia," the detective said.

"Right," Sedgewick said. "He probably planned to go on welfare as soon as he could get to the city. Basil threatened to put a crimp in his plans, and so he killed him. God knows who would have been next. It's a good thing you people are here."

"Yes," said the detective. "Isn't it? Okay, then, we'll check his papers, and if they aren't in order, I guess we'll take him in, though I can't say I buy your theory a hundred percent. I don't suppose you know of any other illegals on the premises, do you? If we check one guy's papers, it almost seems as though we ought to check them all."

"Why?"

"Simple fairness."

"I don't see—" As Sedgewick began to bluster, the two uniformed officers appeared at the top of the stairs with the alien between them, each gripping an elbow. His dark hood was down around his shoulders, revealing a handsome, well-shaped head, now sadly drooping. His eyes were reddened as though from weeping. His hands were cuffed behind his back. They paused on the landing, looking down at the crowd of guests. Father Bingley realized where he had seen this man before, and it caused the very hair to stand up on the back of his neck.

"Death!" he cried, before he could stop himself. "It's Death!" *Why am I trembling?* He tried to explain. "I mean, that's the monk I saw in the library last night." Of course he hadn't seen his face clearly, but that would have been because it was dark, and he was so very black.

Everyone was staring.

"Did you see this man in the guesthouse library last night?" the detective asked him.

"Yes. He was sitting right over there, next to that bloodstain." Father Bingley pointed to the place where he had nearly put his foot in the blood.

"What bloodstain?"

It was gone. "Imagine that," said Father Bingley. "Someone appears to have cleaned it up." He picked up the stool, examined its legs, and squinted at the grout in the tile.

"You're saying there was a bloodstain here?" the detective asked.

"Right here," Father Bingley said. "Not an hour ago." He looked up at the detective, who was working his jaw muscles in an odd way. He was clearly unhappy that the stain had been cleaned up. Father Bingley was reminded of a film he had seen recently on cable TV, one of those premium channels. In that film the detective would give vent to his frustration by shouting the f-word. Movie detectives always swore when they were thwarted. Or in the old days, the days of black and white movies, the detective would throw his fedora on the floor and stamp on it.

But Detective O'Rourke wore no fedora, and cursing on the job must still be considered unprofessional even in these modern times, particularly in a monastery. A certain tightening of the jaw muscles was all that betrayed his displeasure.

"I don't know what happened to the stain," Father Bingley said. "I didn't clean it up."

Only when Jonathan Newmont pushed past the others and began gleefully capturing every angle of the footstool on his videocamera did the detective finally speak, in a low growl: "Get the fuck out of here, kid." The boy ducked away, as though accustomed to the hostile attentions of law officers. That was it, of course. One didn't curse at clergymen. One cursed at young boys. As Father Bingley sorted these sociological observations in his mind, the detective shooed him aside and began to encircle the area around the footstool with yellow and black plastic tape.

Some of the other police personnel came back inside. Detective O'Rourke sent them back out again for testing equipment. Brother Mortimer appeared out of the crowd. "I mopped up the stain," he said. "It's what I do. I see a mess, and I clean it. Did I do wrong?"

"It was a crime scene," Detective O'Rourke said. "We generally like people to leave those alone."

"Oh," said the monk.

"We'll have to talk about this," the detective said. "Save the rag or the mop or whatever it was you used. I'll see you in ten minutes."

"I'll be in the kitchen," said Mortimer.

"Charlie. You got a big bag? Put this footstool in it," the detective said, and continued in this way, giving directions, making notes, while the flashbulbs popped and technicians bustled about.

Martha came and took Father Bingley by the arm. "Let's

go up to our room, dear," she said, "and let these nice officers get on with their work."

The police were taking the little black monk away. He was weeping silently, tears making tracks down his smooth dark cheeks.

"Poor little fellow," Martha said. "Whatever did you mean, calling him 'Death'?"

Father Bingley felt shame. Certainly the monk didn't look threatening now; he looked like a sad child. *Things are different in the middle of the night,* he told himself.

"Nerves," he said to her. "I'm sorry."

"Shouldn't we try to help him somehow?" Martha said.

But someone else was helping him, someone who would perhaps be of more use than a tired, nervous old clergyman; it was Martine Wellworth, Mother Grey's friend, the lawyer. Clearly a lawyer was what he needed.

She was giving him a business card and advising him not to talk to anyone until she could be with him. "I'll be along as soon as I can, Christophe," she said. To Officer Case she said, "What is my client charged with?"

"Murder. We already read him his rights."

"And where are you taking him?"

"Vandervliet City Hall," said Case. "The police station is down in the cellar. You can't miss it."

"I'll see you soon," she said to Christophe. She patted his shoulder, then turned and went up the stairs.

The levels of noise and light in the library were approaching the point of discomfort, police floodlights, police babble. Martha had Father Bingley by the arm and was urging him toward the stairs and upward. He was not sorry to go. Other guests, too, were headed for their rooms, and in the press and jostle, Father Bingley bumped into Rodman Sedgewick, looming above him. It was like jostling a brick wall.

"Excuse me," he said, but the burly politician ignored him and charged onward. Good, then. He never even felt it.

Father Bingley wondered, and not for the first time, whether it was possible for him to make any sort of impression on Sedgewick. Mrs. Sedgewick was a wonderful woman, but after years of association, Father Bingley was beginning to think there was some essential element lacking in Sedgewick himself. Sedgewick seemed to feel these days that Father Bingley could not help him politically, and so his priestly requests for financial assistance went unheeded as often as not. Pointed as he might make them, Father Bingley's sermons never seemed to alter Sedgewick's behavior. Now even physically bumping into him had no effect. He imagined flinging himself bodily at the man and bouncing off like a tennis ball.

Women were more likely to get Sedgewick's attention. Miss Newmont, for instance, young enough to be his daughter. Rounding the corner of the stairs, Father Bingley verified that the reason for Rodman Sedgewick's hasty charge up the stairway was indeed an attractive young woman. Sedgewick had been chasing Martine Wellworth, and now he had her cornered.

"Excuse me, Mrs. Wellworth, but I wonder whether you're aware that the custom at Maitland, Sedgewick, and Grubb is to ask the firm's permission before undertaking a pro bono case." For an instant the image of the two of them was overlaid in Father Bingley's mind with a picture of Simon Legree menacing Little Eva. He could see Sedgewick with a planter's hat, maybe a bullwhip. The muscles in his thick neck bulged.

It's nothing to do with me, Father Bingley thought, and yet he cleared his throat meaningfully. Sedgewick's eyes never flickered.

Mrs. Wellworth did not lend herself quite so readily to

the image of the cowed slave as Sedgewick did to that of the evil overseer. She drew herself up defiantly and shook off the hand he had placed on her arm. "I am aware of the policy toward pro bono cases, Mr. Sedgewick," she said. "The same was true at Sneckman, Flammis even before the merger."

"And yet you seem to be proposing to accept that penniless illegal alien as a client."

She favored him with a cool stare. "Why, yes, Mr. Sedgewick, I believe I am."

"I take it, then, that you're no longer interested in working for Sneckman, Flammis, Flammis, and Wray."

"Not even one little bit," she said.

"Is that so" was all he could find to say, whereupon he turned an interesting color of red, went into his room (St. Barnabas), and slammed the door, rattling the frosted glass.

Father Bingley went to his own room then. Martha had already stripped the bed and thrown the sheets and pillowcases in a pile on the floor.

"I just don't know," she was muttering. The suitcases were open on the bare mattress. As she rummaged in the bureau drawers, it occurred to Father Bingley that she must be quite upset by this whole business.

"Let me help you with the packing, my dear," he offered. Her smile was wonderful to see.

Mother Grey and Deedee sat on the bed in the room called St. Cuthbert, working on solving the murder. Mother Grey favored setting some subtle trap, while Deedee argued that the murderer's identity would be blindingly apparent if only they could complete the construction of a timeline chart showing all relevant events of the night in question. Mother Grey could not make head or tail of Deedee's chart.

On the other hand, she was having trouble producing a good plan for a trap.

Suddenly Martine barged in. "I think I just cut my own professional throat," she said.

"What happened?" Mother Grey said, laying aside her note pad, which bore only a few doodles in the shape of mousetraps.

"I refused to back down to Sedgewick about taking Christophe's case. But you know, I'd do it again."

"What did he do, fire you?" Deedee said.

"If it wasn't that, it would have been something else," Martine said.

"Can you take his case? Don't you have to be licensed to practice law in New York?" Mother Grey asked.

"I am. New York, New Jersey, Pennsylvania, Delaware, and Connecticut," Martine said, with what looked to Mother Grey like something of a swagger. And why not? She was a remarkable woman. Imagine passing all those bar exams. "I need the keys to the minivan, Deedee, if it's okay," Martine added. "I have to go into the village and meet with my client."

"Certainly," Deedee said. "Here. But Martine, what are you going to do? You and your husband are both out of work now."

"Both out of work. Except that I have this interesting pro bono case. You know, I've been wanting to get into immigration law. Sneckman, Flammis was never going to offer me any opportunities in that line." Humming a little tune, she headed out the door.

"I hope they have some savings," Mother Grey said.

"It's possible to live without a lot of money," Deedee said. "As you know."

"As I know too well," Mother Grey said. "But voluntary simplicity isn't something I ever thought Martine would want to try." Still, Martine looked happier than she had seen her in a long time.

"It's this place," Deedee said. "It's the influence of this place."

Yes, and now they were stuck here, Mother Grey realized, without so much as a car. Was this how it felt to be a monk, immured forever, miles from every worldly gratification? No. The lives of these men were rich, and they had chosen them willingly. She glanced guiltily at the icon of Jesus over the dresser.

8

"Here's the timeline," said Deedee. She opened the black and white composition book on the bedspread next to Mother Grey. "Now, pay attention. Sometime shortly after midnight, Delight sees Christophe and Basil carrying the chest."

"Poor old dear."

"Twelve-ten, Sedgewick gets up—because of a headache, he says—and sees nobody, he says, while Ouida sees a monklike figure going into somebody's room, she says."

"You don't suppose . . ."

"She thinks it was her husband, I bet a hat. She thinks he was visiting Beryl Newmont."

"Which would take care of both their alibis, if true," Mother Grey said. "Rats. There goes Sedgewick as a suspect."

"Might not be all that airtight," Deedee said. "We can ask them about it."

"Do you really think they would give us honest answers?"

"Never mind that, the truth will come out if we apply ourselves to the facts. Then, around midnight, Father Bingley gets up, goes downstairs, and sees Christophe, or someone like him, sitting all alone in the dark in the library."

"Who knows what he saw?" Mother Grey said. "It was dark, after all."

"He seemed pretty sure of himself this morning," Deedee said. " 'Death, Death.' "

"It was to puke. Wait a minute," Mother Grey said. "If I could mistake Sedgewick for Basil in broad daylight, why couldn't someone else have mistaken Basil for Sedgewick in the dark? Or for someone else? What if the killing were a case of mistaken identity?"

"You think someone killed Basil in mistake for Rodman Sedgewick."

"I mistook him for Basil this morning. It could have worked the other way around."

"It certainly gives us a wealth of suspects."

"Ouida in a fit of jealousy."

"Martine."

"Martine would kill him in an instant, Deedee, but she would never use one of Delight van Buskirk's knitting needles."

"Maybe that's what she counted on our thinking. But if we admit mistaken identity, Vinnie, we have to add you as a suspect."

"Me?"

"Yes. You stabbed him, thinking he was Bingley."

"I would never stab Bingley in the back, Deedee. Never. I would want to see his face. Here's an idea: Maybe

Sedgewick wasn't the only one here with a garment resembling a monk's robe. We should search everyone's luggage."

"You're serious."

"Just to see who might have resembled Basil in the dark, or who Basil might have resembled."

"Whom," said Deedee. It was noon; they heard the bell ring for diurnum.

"Are they continuing with the offices, then?" Mother Grey asked.

"Yes, Fergus says they're going to carry on normally. The library will be off-limits, as will the part of the grounds where Basil was found, but apart from that everything is to go on as before." Footsteps in the hall told them the guests were on their way to the noonday service.

"While they're all at diurnum, we should split up and search their rooms," said Mother Grey.

"Right," said Deedee. They waited until the last footfall had died away.

Since there were no locks on the doors of the rooms with the names of saints, it was a simple matter for Mother Grey and Deedee to go through the guest rooms for monks' robes; simple, that is, if you didn't count nervous guilt as a complication. Mother Grey took a note pad and pencil and made careful swift sketches of everything she found in the way of a robe or long floppy garment, noting the room name and the owner.

Every room had a bed, a holy picture, and a chest of drawers. In St. Columba the face of Our Lord gazed reprovingly at Mother Grey out of an austere frame over the chest. The drawers were empty. Beryl Newmont was living out of her suitcase; how tacky. It stood open beside the unmade bed. She slipped her hand under the pile of slithery frillies on the bottom and found a piece of paper.

Glossy paper, folded, plain white, with torn edges. She unfolded it and beheld a likeness of Rodman Sedgewick.

Printed in black and white, the photograph looked like a formal portrait. He was sitting in what appeared to be one of the library chairs here at the monastery, one wingtip hooked over the low footrail, with a woman's arm around his shoulder. The part of the picture showing the woman had been torn off. A bit of red, white, and blue border showed at the torn edge of the picture.

It must have come from a campaign poster from the time he ran for senator. The arm would have belonged to Ouida; even in these free-spirited days, men running for high office did not customarily publish pictures of themselves in the embrace of women other than their wives.

Scrawled across the picture in an overwrought hand were the words, "Yes! Yes!! Yes!!!"

Put it back or take it? *I want Deedee to see this,* she thought. *Then if we decide to put it back, we'll put it back.*

On the bed was a burgundy robe with a hood. She made a note of it and moved on to St. Sebastian, Jonathan Newmont's room.

In a bureau drawer, next to a pile of blank tapes and extra batteries, Mother Grey found a stash of marijuana and rolling papers, wrapped up in a long brown robe. "A habit," she muttered, though not quite the evidence they were seeking.

Still, the long brown robe.

Who were these people? Why had they come here? To make a doper movie? Surely this boy could have found just as much profit staying home and getting stoned in Rolling Hills, taking pictures of his friends, if any. Perhaps his sister had brought him here to straighten him out. It didn't seem to be working.

Mother Grey was tossing the last room just as the worshipers began to return from diurnum. It was Martine's room, and Martine was in Vandervliet-on-Hudson trying to help the luckless Christophe. So all she had to do was stand away from the glass of the door and wait for the crowd to pass.

Except that not all of the crowd went past. The doorknob rattled. She jumped behind the window drapery—floor-length in this room, luckily, made of pale gray monk's cloth and decorated at the bottom with a chaste stencil of plant forms in rust and green.

"Oooh, *Roger.*" Sounds of kissing and the muffled snapping of a bra strap. It was the Smartts.

"Come on, come on. Off with those pants."

"Not here!"

"Yes, here. Why not? Martine won't be back for hours."

"Someone might come in to clean. Ow! Let go." Why on earth couldn't these tiresome people have gone to the Poconos to enjoy their conjugal bliss in one of the fabled heart-shaped beds, like normal lovers?

"Off with them," Roger Smartt said. There was a scuffle, and a lot of giggling, and then the sound of breaking glass as a bottle fell to the floor. Rose reek filled the room. The Smartts must have knocked over Martine's cologne.

They fled. No doubt they feared the sudden appearance of Brother Mortimer with his broom.

As soon as the Smartts were out of sight, Mother Grey followed, stepping in the rose cologne and tracking whiffs of it down the hall. Deedee was waiting in St. Anselm, where they had agreed to meet with their findings.

"Pee-you," said Deedee. "What did you get into?"

Did she smell as bad as all that? "The Smartts were getting rowdy in Martine's room and broke her cologne. I stepped in it. You know, I have serious doubts about those people's motives in coming here this weekend. And certain other people's too."

"Next time we won't invite the Smartts," Deedee said. "What did you find?"

"This," she said, producing the torn campaign poster. Deedee took it and marveled.

"She must really be stuck on the old goat," Deedee said. "No accounting for tastes, I suppose."

"And here are my notes on the various garments I found. Shall we skip lunch to go over them?"

"I never work on an empty stomach," Deedee declared.

The police were still all over the library, but they allowed the guests to file through on their way to the refectory. Deedee and Mother Grey took their food to a far corner, putting three tables of chattering youngsters between themselves and the people they regarded as suspects. Thus shielded from prying and possibly guilty eyes and ears, they spread the results of their efforts next to the plates of fried chicken. Deedee had gotten hold of a big piece of graph paper from somewhere.

Now that things weren't quite so hectic, Mother Grey found time to note down that Martine's bathrobe was a loud black and white plaid. That certainly settled the question of whether Martine had been creeping about like a monk in the night. "What did you bring to wear back and forth to the bathroom, by the way, Deedee?"

"Pink chenille."

"Really!"

"A very deep pink chenille, Vinnie, almost like fuschia. It's not as though I were a pastel sort of person." She bit off a piece of chicken leg, chewed it carefully, and swallowed. "And you?"

"Dark blue flannel."

"The cut?"

"It's bathrobe shape, rounded lapels with no notches, calf-length with a tie belt." And three small moth-holes, she reflected, but this was hardly to the point.

She examined Deedee's list of garments while Deedee examined hers. Bingley's bathrobe (white), Martha's bathrobe (flowered), Roger Smartt (a monk's habit), Sedgewick's bathrobe (pale yellow terry), Ouida's (a striped caftan), Annabelle Smartt (fake leopard), Delight van Buskirk (quilted pink satin), B. Newmont's bathrobe (burgundy with a hood), Jonathan's bathrobe (dark brown with a floppy collar), Martine's robe (black and white plaid), Deedee (fuschia chenille), Vinnie (navy flannel).

"What did you mean by this?" Mother Grey demanded. " 'Roger Smartt, St. Augustine, a monk's habit.' What kind of a bathrobe was it?"

"It wasn't a bathrobe, I tell you, it was a monk's habit. I know one when I see one. It had the big hood, the floppy sleeves. It was your standard monk's habit."

"I see. What color?"

"White."

"But why would he bring a monk's robe here? Was it just like the robes the monks wear, or—"

"It was, I don't know, a little lighter, part polyester instead of all linen or sackcloth or whatever it is the guys wear. Come to think of it, maybe it could have been an alb."

"An alb?"

"I don't know, Vinnie. It was white, it was long, it was floppy."

"One of the albs from St. Bede's?"

"You know your own parishioners best."

"He stole one of my albs?"

"I'm not sure that's what it was. Don't get upset. Here, we'll just put him down on the list as having access to a garment that could make him look like a monk."

And so Deedee made two lists, one of those who had access to garments, either dark or light, that would have made them look monklike in the night, and those who, as far as they knew, did not. Mother Grey put aside the question of Roger Smartt and the alb for the present.

Nearly everybody was on the first list.

Using both lists and her notes from the interview of that morning, Deedee filled the graph paper with indecipherable scrawls. Mother Grey was unable to visualize anything at all by means of the graph.

"We've left out the most important thing," she said.

"What?"

"What was it these people wore on their feet?"

"Nobody said."

"When he's all swaddled up, it's how you tell one monk from another. For instance, Octavian wears boating moccasins, Basil wore suede lace-up shoes or sandals. Bunny slippers would have been me," said Mother Grey.

"We'll have to go back to the witnesses and ask them, one by one. Even at that, you know, the only thing you can say for sure about the people who were seen in white monk's garb is that they were potential victims, in the mistaken-identity theory. The killer could have been wearing white robes, black robes, or anything else."

"Oh, squat," said Mother Grey. Her head was beginning to swim.

"I'm going to take a nap," said Deedee. "Maybe the answer will come to me in my sleep. I'll see you later."

"Give me the notebook, then," said Mother Grey.

Lunch was over. The police were gone from the library, and the guests were free to use it once more. Still, Mother Grey went back to her room.

She closed the door and got busy with her nail scissors, cutting out paper dolls. Her plan was to move them around in a conceptual model of the monastery. Only in this way could she see who was where and with whom on the fatal night.

Dark robes, light robes. As she stood the figures up on the dresser (representing the upstairs hall) it suddenly struck her that people could change clothes. What she needed was to cut the little robes out separately, with tabs on the shoulders, in case she needed to make believe they changed over from white to black or vice versa. It was excessively complicated this way, but she did it just the same, not wanting to rule out any reasonable possibilities.

Now the paper dolls could all go parading down to the refectory (represented by the top drawer), or barge into one another's rooms, or go to the loo. Here in the black robe was Christophe, resting in the library after carrying the heavy chest. Here, in white, was Father Bingley. *Slowly he comes down the stairs.*

A light knock at the door; a clearing of the throat. Fergus was out there.

"I found Basil's journal," he said. "I thought you and Deedee might want to have a look at it before I gave it to the police." He glanced over her shoulder at the little paper monks but did not remark upon them.

"Where is it?" she said, holding his gaze.

"In my office downstairs. You and Deedee can meet me there before vespers, and I'll show it to you. I'll see you in five minutes." He closed the door and left, but not before Mother Grey had a look at his feet, still thinking of shoes as clues. Crepe-soled brogues. Very quiet. She made a note of it in the book.

Deedee woke up at once. "He found the diary? What's it like? Does Basil say, 'Dear diary,' and stuff like that?"

"No telling," said Mother Grey. "We have to go down to his office and see it for ourselves. Come on."

On the stairs they ran into the Smartts, headed toward their rooms, both in running clothes.

"Wait!" said Mother Grey. "I need to ask you some things about last night."

"Last night?" said Annabelle.

"You mean, last night, when we were safely asleep in our cold separate beds?" said Roger.

"Whatever," said Deedee, giving them a suspicious look. Annabelle edged away from her, fearing perhaps to get snapped behind the ear again.

"Anyway, we need to know some things," Mother Grey said. "First, did you get up out of bed last night? And if so, did you see anyone else in the hall, or notice the time? Also we need to know what you were wearing." *Furthermore, did you happen to murder an old monk and drag his body out into the weeds while you were up?*

And where do you get off pinching my alb?

"I didn't get up. Did you get up, Annabelle?"

"No, I didn't get up. Didn't get up, didn't see a thing."

"Slept like a rock," said Roger.

"Two rocks," said Annabelle. "Sorry we can't help you." They sidled past and continued on upstairs.

"They're lying," said Deedee. "Why are they lying?"

"Because they're slimy people," said Mother Grey. "They don't respect anything that goes on here."

"They're your parishioners, not mine," said Deedee. "Thank goodness."

"Time to apply some firm pastoral guidance," Mother Grey said.

"Right," said Deedee. "But first the diary. So what do you think? Will it reveal the dark secret of Rodman Sedgewick's mysterious past?"

"His mother was a Democrat. His mother was an actress."

"Do you suppose he kept pictures? In his wallet, perhaps. Here's what, Vinnie—if the diary doesn't tell us anything, you can distract him with your womanly wiles while I lift his wallet. After that we can go through it till we come to an old baby picture, Rodman Sedgewick in his mother's arms. Then we'll know the truth."

"People don't carry old baby pictures of themselves in their wallets. Especially if they contain a secret they want to keep from their wives."

"Did you hear he was buying a weekly newspaper?"

"Yes, with Ouida's money," said Mother Grey. "I think he plans to get into molding public opinion."

"Too bad for him that nobody reads anymore," Deedee said. "What was it Basil was saying to him when he knocked over the dishes? 'You were the first one of your—' "

"Sexual orientation?"

"IQ, maybe. First boy with an IQ lower than a hundred admitted to St. Botolph's."

Out of the corner of her eye, Mother Grey saw balls of yarn all over the library floor, spilling out from behind a bookcase. "What's this?" she said.

Peculiar. Yarn balls all over the floor. They ran down the stairs to follow the trail, and there behind the bookcase lay Delight van Buskirk, her skin horribly pale, the thin plastic yarn ball bag pulled all the way over her head.

9

"I want to go home. I want to go home right now. I've had enough of this."

Mrs. van Buskirk had recovered her breath at last and was giving vent to her feelings. They had found her and removed the plastic bag just in time. As Mother Grey prepared to give mouth-to-mouth resuscitation, the old lady coughed, spluttered, and began to complain in a loud voice. Now the monks were standing in a circle, praying over her.

"Somebody please take me home," she said.

"Mrs. van Buskirk, someone tried to kill you," Fergus said.

"I know it. I'm tired of it. Get me out of here."

"Did you see who it was?"

"No."

"What happened?"

"Strong hands seized me from behind." *She's been reading those novels again,* Mother Grey thought.

"Men's hands or women's hands?" Deedee asked.

Mother Grey said, "Did you smell anything, or sense anything—"

"I want to go home, I tell you, and I want to go home right now. Is anyone going to take me out of this wretched place?"

Deedee promised to drive her to the train station in Poughkeepsie as soon as the police had finished talking to her.

"She can't go on the train alone," said Mother Grey.

"We'll go with her," said Roger Smartt. "We're all packed." He smiled, the ever-helpful Boy Scout.

The others stared at him. Many suspected him of attacking the old lady. Though no one was impolite enough to come right out and accuse him, their faces spoke volumes.

Smartt was stunned, or gave a good imitation of it. "Hey, you're not thinking— Come on, you couldn't believe that I—"

"Somebody did this, and it wasn't Christophe," Deedee said. "I don't think any of us should leave without talking to the police first."

"I should," said Mrs. van Buskirk. "I should leave right now. I have to get out of here." She got up and started for the door. Mother Grey was hanging on her arm; she shook her off. "I'll be waiting in the van if anyone wants me. You can send my things later."

"Dear, you must talk to the police. Please wait," Mother Grey said.

"Then I'll be sitting in the vestibule. Can someone call me a taxi?"

"The police would probably be very unhappy to have to follow you back to New Jersey," said Fergus. "That's true of everyone here, by the way. Mother Grey is right." He put his arm around Mrs. van Buskirk. "Come with me. We'll keep you safe."

Mother Grey and Deedee further surrounded the old lady, and they ushered her, still complaining, through the hall and into Fergus's office.

As Fergus dialed the police, Mrs. van Buskirk said, "Can you please lock the door?"

"Do you remember anything about the person who attacked you?" Mother Grey asked.

"No." Mrs. van Buskirk took a seat in the corner, away from the window. "I'll just sit here with my back to the wall."

Fergus frowned and looked through his desk for the key. "This door hasn't been kept locked since St. Hugh's was a boys' school," he said. The police dispatcher came on the line, and Fergus relayed the details of the monastery's latest troubles.

"One thing you might do, Mrs. van Buskirk, is tell us whatever you know that would make someone want to keep you quiet," Deedee said. "Then you'd be perfectly safe, because there would be no point to it anymore. Assuming that this was the motive behind your attack."

"What could I know? I'm just an old lady."

"Something about Rodman Sedgewick," Mother Grey suggested. Fergus gave her a sharp look. *Leading the witness.*

"Something about anybody here," Deedee said. "Or something you saw last night that you haven't remembered to mention."

"I told Brother Fergus everything I saw. You people told me I was dreaming. Maybe I was dreaming, I don't know."

"Somebody didn't think so," said Mother Grey.

"What about the person who attacked you? Can you remember anything at all? A smell? A feeling?"

"Yes—no—I don't know. There *was* something. I remembered it a minute ago, but now it's gone. Just get me home. I'll be fine."

Fergus hung up. "They're on their way," he said. "By the way, here's Basil's journal."

"Lock the door, will you?" said Deedee. "Or have you found the key yet?"

"Yes, here it is," he said. The hardware for locking the door was one of those old-timey keyhole-shaped keyholes, and the key that worked it was the sort of skeleton key you could pick up at any hardware store—hardly proof against sophisticated burglars, but then, who encountered sophisticated burglars out here? There was nothing to steal. The treasures of St. Hugh's were laid up in Heaven, where moth doth not corrupt. The key squeaked in the old lock.

"Hope we can open that again," said Fergus. "Maybe I should have oiled it."

Nevertheless the gesture gave them a sense of safety. Secure at last from attempts on the old lady's life and other interruptions, they gathered around Basil's journal, like bomb squad experts eyeing a suspicious package.

Deedee was the first to touch it.

She picked it up. "It's just like my notebook," she said, and it was, a black-and-white-mottled composition book with the pages sewn in.

"They're cheap," said Fergus. "We're sworn to poverty."

She opened it and riffled through. Mother Grey and Mrs. van Buskirk crowded together to peer over her shoulder.

Basil's handwriting was clear and remarkably steady for someone so elderly. The entries were short, three or four on a page. Most had to do with Basil's prayer life and spiritual development, but every so often he commented on what he had done or whom he had seen that day, or made a note on the weather.

For instance, he recorded that it rained a lot in sub-Saharan Africa. His sketchy account of their travels from the dark continent never mentioned Christophe, hiding in the chest the whole way. What else had he left unsaid? What use was this miserable diary? It told them nothing. *God is good, yes, yes, God is good. But we knew that already, Basil, dear.*

Deedee flipped on. The entries increasingly were complaints about Basil's bodily aches and pains. They came to the last page with writing on it, and then—wouldn't you know it!—a ragged edge where a page had been torn out.

"Why has the last page been torn out?" Mother Grey said.

Fergus rubbed his chin. "Perhaps he wrote something and then repented of it. Perhaps he didn't want anyone to see it. Basil was very old. Few as his possessions were, he knew that he was going to have to abandon them to others soon."

"Or the killer ripped it out while you were out of your office, looking after Mrs. van Buskirk."

On the chance that such a killer would be so simple as to cast the torn fragment into Fergus's wastebasket, Mother Grey upended it, but nothing came out except three used tissues and a little nervous ball of gray hair. Fergus's hair, probably. He was still pulling at it.

Fergus kept no ashtray; they had noticed no lingering smell of burning in the office. "Maybe he still has the diary page on him," said Deedee.

"Or she," Mother Grey said.

"I wish we could search Sedgewick's pockets," Deedee muttered.

"Why Sedgewick?" Fergus said. "What are these dark hints?"

"Our prime suspect, so far," Deedee said.

"What makes you suspect Rodman Sedgewick?" said Fergus. "His wife is a patron of the monastery. They've been coming here for years. Why do you think he would suddenly begin to murder the monks?"

"Basil was his teacher," Mother Grey said. "He knew something about him that Sedgewick wanted kept quiet."

"You know, dear, it would be a simple matter to search Rodman Sedgewick's things," said Delight van Buskirk. They had forgotten she was there.

"How do you figure?" Deedee said.

"Go through his things while he's in the shower."

"Suppose he isn't taking a shower?"

"He's already taken one this morning," said Mother Grey.

"Force him to take another one. Tell him he stinks," the old lady suggested.

Deedee said, "He knows he stinks, he's a—"

"No lawyer jokes, please," Mother Grey murmured. "Have some respect for our friend Martine."

"Do something to make him stink, then. Throw something smelly on him. The sooner I'm back in Fishersville, the happier I'll be."

Fergus put his head in his hands. "This is not my idea of the Lord's work," he said. Ignoring him, the women compiled, with considerable relish, a list of stinky things they could get hold of and throw all over Rodman Sedgewick. Dead fish. Manure. Insecticide. Bad eggs.

"Rose perfume," said Mother Grey, thinking of her shoe.

"What would we do? Walk up and squirt him with rose perfume? Might make him suspicious," Deedee said.

"It doesn't sound like something two clergywomen in their right minds would do," Fergus said.

"Anyway, we don't have any," Mother Grey said. "The Smartts broke Martine's bottle of it."

"I heard of a dodge with mustard that pickpockets used to work at the airport," Deedee said. "Or was it molesters in the supermarket? I can't recall."

"Whatever we do, we'd better do it quick before he gets rid of the diary page," Mother Grey said.

"If it was he who took it," Fergus said.

"Right. If it was he."

"As we speak, he could be putting it down the toilet," Mrs. van Buskirk said.

"Let's go," Mother Grey said.

They left Mrs. van Buskirk with Fergus, behind the securely locked office door.

The first person they saw in the library was Annabelle Smartt, sitting by the door filing her nails, right there in public. Granny would have fainted at the sight.

"Where's Sedgewick?" Mother Grey demanded.

Annabelle uncrossed her legs and crossed them the other way, then inclined her head toward the hallway that led to the refectory. "He's talking to the woman with the hair."

"Good," said Mother Grey. Deedee snatched up Annabelle's half-empty coffee mug, and the two clergywomen paraded across the library and into the front hall.

The heavy door to the refectory was open, propped against the wall; Sedgewick had Berry Newmont with her mane of yellow curls backed up against it. He was not quite touching her, but his arm was up against the door in such a way as to block retreat as he assaulted her with some political tirade. She held her coffee mug between them like a shield.

"Not the flat tax again," Mother Grey muttered.

"On three," said Deedee. "We crowd in the door and spill her coffee on him. One—two—"

No gang of airport pickpockets could have done it better.

Sedgewick's scream of distress told them that Berry Newmont's coffee was still hot, not like Annabelle's, which Deedee managed to pour on his head under the guise of helping him as he stooped over to pick up Newmont's cup.

"I'm so sorry," she said. "Please let me—"

"It's all right," he said, fending her off. "I'll just go wash off and change." He rushed out and through the library.

Casting a glance at the women that clearly said she thought them a pair of dangerous lunatics, Berry Newmont retreated to the refectory, probably for more coffee. Brother Mortimer came out of the kitchen with his mop and followed Sedgewick all the way across the library and up the stairs, cleaning up the drips.

Hard on his heels came Mother Grey and Deedee, avoiding the wet spots. *My word*, thought Mother Grey. *What if he takes off his clothes in the men's room?* They needed a male confederate. Perhaps Mortimer—

But no, their plan had worked perfectly. As Mortimer came down the steps, they went up, and when they reached the top, Sedgewick's robe-clad back was disappearing through the door to the men's room. He had taken his clothes off.

In the room called St. Barnabas, the bed had been freshly made, doubtless by Ouida, and the bags were neatly stacked next to the door. One case was unzipped, the one from which Sedgewick had retrieved his robe. A sad heap of sticky clothing lay in the middle of the floor.

"Wonder who he thinks will pick these up?" Deedee muttered. She took up the pants, a pair of khakis bearing a label on the back pocket that said "Duck Head" with a little embroidered mallard, and fumbled around in the pockets. What she sought was in the left-side front.

"Bingo," she said.

They smoothed out the brown-stained composition book

page, and there was Basil's neat handwriting, perfectly legible if a little runny.

The arthritis is worse and worse, and I find myself thinking that if I only had a good chair in here instead of this hard chest, I could continue my studies for much longer at a stretch.

I was longing to ask R.S. today whether his mother was happy after the family left the continent. Such a lovely woman. One hears of so many interracial marriages failing when the expatriates return to the States.

"Interracial?" Mother Grey repeated.

"'The first student at St. Botolph's of your race,'" said Deedee. "That's what Basil was going to say, when Sedgewick dropped the cups." Suddenly it made perfect sense, Rodman Sedgewick's dark secret.

"Sedgewick's mother was African American," said Mother Grey. "Or African. Some sort of nonwhite person."

Deedee frowned. "How could this have escaped the notice of his society friends? I'm sure such things were very important when he was young, just starting out in the law, and politics."

"I don't know, Deedee. As Delight van Buskirk said, nobody in New Jersey knew the family while his mother was still alive, and after that—you know how it is with East Coast Wasps. They communicate in wordless signals."

"No, I don't. Tell me, what sort of wordless signal would indicate that a man's mother was a woman of color? I've never traveled in those circles," said Deedee.

"Nothing as specific as 'His mother was a woman of color.' More a generic signal indicating something not right, the same one they would use if his father were a Jew, or he gambled away all his money, or his show dog had only one testicle."

"How does it go? I want to see it."

"It's been so long since I traveled in those circles myself that I don't really remember. I think it was done with one eyebrow and a slight clearing of the throat."

"Hem-hem," Deedee attempted. It didn't look quite right. "But, wait," she said. "Now he's Rodman Sedgewick, king of the county horse set. How did he get from there to here?"

"Years passed. Maybe the exact meaning of the signal was forgotten, since nobody came right out and spoke of it. He graduated from the right schools, he spoke with the right accent, he sat a horse beautifully, and he married bales of money. So we didn't care anymore what it was about him."

"Hm. All this is too much for me, Vinnie. I'm Irish. We say what we think right out."

"Yes, when you want people to know what you think. At other times you say what you want people to think you think."

Deedee gave her a look, perhaps pondering whether to take up the gauntlet, but then she let it go. "Okay, so Sedgewick's father remarries. The second wife is the heiress to a great fortune."

"Or a tidy horse farm, anyhow," Mother Grey said.

"Whatever. Still, none of it necessarily goes to Sedgewick on his stepmother's death. But Ouida is very comfortably off indeed. So she and Sedgewick marry."

"Meanwhile Ouida has no idea—"

"None at all," Deedee breathed, madly making notes. She was in ecstasies. A family saga!

"Ouida has no idea of what?" They looked up, and there stood the woman herself, blocking the doorway.

Think fast! Mother Grey urged herself, mentally composing the first few bars of a song and dance she could deliver without actually lying. The effort was unnecessary; at once Ouida spotted the Duck Head khakis dangling from

Deedee's guilty hands and was off on an entirely different tack.

"What are you doing with my husband's trousers!?" she demanded.

"Ah. These. We found them on the floor in the hall," Deedee said. "Those teenagers must have dragged the clothes around when they were looking through the up- stairs. Can you imagine? As I was just saying to Vinnie, I'm sure you had no idea they were out there." She tucked the diary page into her own pocket. "Otherwise you would have picked them up."

"What was that you just put in your pocket?"

"Something of mine," Deedee said. "It has nothing to do with anything."

"Really."

"Nothing at all. So here are Rodman's pants," said Deedee.

"Thank you," Ouida said, not looking in the least grateful.

"See ya." As the two clergywomen left the room called St. Barnabas, Deedee looked back at Ouida, raised one eye- brow slightly, and cleared her throat. This time she must have got the inflection right. Ouida looked mad enough to kill her.

In the narrow hallway Roger Smartt slithered past them—furtively, Mother Grey thought—carrying three bags: one masculine-looking valise, a woman's overnight case, and a hatbox of some sort. There was an air about him of one who is accustomed to leaving hotels without letting the front desk know he was going.

It was Deedee who challenged him. "Where are you off to?"

"Just thought I'd pack the car," Roger said.

"It's locked," Deedee said.

"It is?"

"Yes, you'll need the key," Deedee said. "I'll come down with you and let you in. Let me help with that." Before he could divine her intent, she seized the valise, tugging it sharply from his grip, and whacked it against the wall as though by mistake. "Oh, mercy me, what have I done? I'm so sorry." The lid fell open—Mother Grey was almost certain she had fiddled with the catch first—and the contents spewed across the hallway floor.

"Property of St. Bede's, Fishersville" showed clearly where Mother Grey had inked it on the label of Ralph Voercker's old alb. Mother Grey picked it up, saying, "This is mine, I believe." A sweaty odor arose from the garment; it was stained. Roger smirked at her. Before her eyes the image arose unbidden of Roger, bedecked in her alb, enjoying conjugal bliss with Annabelle. Later she thought, *Now why would the misuse of church property make me angrier than the wanton murder of a saintly old monk?* But it wasn't that it made her angrier altogether—it was just that the spike of short-term anger was sharper, catching her off-guard. That must have been why she lost her temper and hit him.

10

"What was that for?" Roger Smartt said. He put his hand to his face. "I haven't been slapped by a girl in thirty years."

"You'd better not call her a girl," Deedee said, "or she'll give you a punch in the stomach."

Mother Grey bit her lip sharply and regained control of herself. Violence! What would Brother Basil have said! "Roger. I'm sorry."

"Think nothing of it," he said. He took his hand away, revealing the red handprint she had left on the side of his face.

"I didn't mean to—I never would have—but you must understand, I feel very, very angry. You and Annabelle have been using this alb, the property of St. Bede's, for kinky sex."

"You're right," he said. "You caught us. I'm sorry. Annabelle thought it would be—I'm sorry. What can I say? I'm—I'm sorry." He backed away from them, headed toward the stairs. "Sorry," he said, and bolted downward. His voice came floating up from the landing: "It will never happen again."

"He got that right, anyway," Mother Grey said. "As soon as I get back I'm locking everything up. I should have done that the last time, when the devil-worshipers got hold of my good black cassock. What are you laughing at?"

"Nothing," Deedee said. "Sorry. I'm sorry."

"You think this is funny?"

"Don't you?"

"No."

Deedee sighed and straightened her face. "It helps with one thing, anyhow; we have a piece of the puzzle—Ouida's lustful midnight monk." She took out her notebook and penciled in Roger's name next to Ouida Sedgewick's reported sighting of a monk in white.

"The nerve," said Mother Grey. "The very idea, bringing their fleshpot mentality to a spiritual retreat. They came here for some sort of weird turn-on, do you realize that? Carrying on all night, carrying on all day. They aren't serious people. I think I'm getting a headache."

"The human inclination to fleshpottiness cannot be denied, Vinnie."

"What the Smartts need is fleshpotty training," Mother Grey muttered.

"They're married, after all, Vinnie."

"Well, okay, maybe they're a little bit funny."

"Try ridiculous. Here's an idea; maybe Roger noticed something in the night, while he was, er, up."

"I can't imagine it. He didn't notice me in Martine's room, did he? And yet there I was, with my sensible brogues poking out from under the curtain, perfectly visible."

"But maybe he noticed what time it was when he was in the hall. That would help our timetable."

"Good thought. We'll ask him."

"Let's ask Annabelle first."

They found Annabelle making Roger's bed in the room called St. Augustine. She looked up and smiled at them. "Imagine putting flat sheets on the bottom," she said. "Where do you suppose they found these flat sheets to put on the bottom? They're just like the top sheets. So old-timey."

"The monks make them out of top sheets," Deedee suggested. "It's a holy work of the Lord."

Annabelle blinked, but before she had time to register the fact that Deedee was pulling her leg, she noticed the alb in Mother Grey's hands. She turned beet red and began to squirm.

"Yes, Annabelle, I know what you and Roger have been up to," Mother Grey said.

"I'm—er—"

"All we want to know is what time it was when Roger came to your room last night," Deedee said. "And whether either of you noticed anything that could help us solve Basil's murder."

"Anything at all," Mother Grey said. "We'll address the problem of the stolen alb at another time." *And anyway I already chastised Roger for it.* Firm pastoral guidance. Not violence. No.

"It was Roger's idea," Annabelle said. "He wanted to make believe he was a monk."

"Spare me the details," said Mother Grey.

"What time was it?" Deedee said. "That's what we need to know."

"Almost fourteen minutes after twelve," Annabelle said. "I remember it particularly because my travel alarm fell off the nightstand when Roger—"

"Never mind Roger," Mother Grey said. "There's just one other thing I need to know."

"What's that?"

"What was he wearing on his feet?"

"On his feet?"

"Right," said Deedee. "You know, like, bedroom slippers, or SS boots, or high-heeled pumps—"

"Nothing," she said.

"Not anything."

"Nothing at all. His feet were completely bare."

"So. What does all this tell us?" Deedee mused. The intrepid clergy-detectives had regrouped in the room called St. Cuthbert, where they sat on the bed with notebook, chart, and paper dolls.

"I don't know," said Mother Grey. "What? You aren't going to bring up the Smartts and their sex life again, are you? I already know more than I care to about that subject."

"No, this is an exercise in logic." She spread out the notebook. "At twelve-thirteen or thereabouts Ouida Sedgewick got up and saw Roger Smartt going into Annabelle's room dressed as a monk, all in white. She seemed to think it was Sedgewick she was seeing, though she wouldn't come out and say so. Then at twelve-fourteen Roger was in Annabelle's bed, making enough noise to wake Martha Bingley, who remarked on it to Father B. Does all this suggest anything to you?"

"It suggests that Bingley was in bed at the time, and that Rodman Sedgewick . . . was not."

"Do you think Bingley went downstairs and saw Christophe after that, or before?"

"I suppose we can always ask him," Mother Grey said, although she had no great hopes of getting a straight answer out of Rupert Bingley. "It would also help to know exactly when Basil was killed."

"We should talk to Mrs. van Buskirk again. Now that her curious story appears to be true, perhaps she might remember noticing the time."

Fergus's Liberia pictures were spread over his desk when Mother Grey and Deedee returned to his office. Fergus pointed to one of them. "The third and fourth from the end are Christophe's parents," he was saying to Detective O'Rourke. "Their heads were found in that pile over there." Mother Grey couldn't look. "These two are his younger sisters," he added.

"Brother Fergus, I'm not an immigration cop. I have no way to process what you're telling me," O'Rourke said.

Fergus looked into O'Rourke's face, focusing on the detective the full force of his own hunger for justice. "Release Christophe. He is not guilty of the attacks here, or else why would they continue, with him in jail?"

"That's up to the judge. Your guy's hearing is tomorrow morning," O'Rourke said. Mother Grey could see that the prior's intensity was beginning to burn through O'Rourke's hard shell. He shifted his weight uncomfortably.

"Surely you're not going to hold Christophe overnight," Deedee said. "After all he's suffered." The Liberia pictures were in color, Mother Grey noted, and looked away again.

O'Rourke shrugged helplessly. "Lady—"

Mrs. van Buskirk spoke up. "Well, you're not taking me anywhere, that's for certain." She stood up and gathered her pocketbook.

"Ma'am, you're going to have to come with me to the emergency room and let the doctors take a look at you." O'Rourke was back on firm moral ground. "Somebody tried to kill you. I have to find out who. If you don't cooperate, it makes it impossible for me to do my job."

"I'm sorry about your job," she said. "But I hate hospitals. And I'm not sick, you know."

"You'll be in and out of there before you know it," he said.

"I'm very glad to have caught you before you left," Mother Grey said to O'Rourke. "Do you mind if I ask you some things about Brother Basil's murder?"

"Such as?"

"Have they established a time of death?"

"I guess it can't hurt to tell you that," O'Rourke said. "The pathologist figures the time of death at somewhere between eleven-thirty and one."

"Can't pin it down any closer than that, eh?" Deedee said.

"Nope. But if you ladies want to play detective, another thing they found during the autopsy was what they thought were the remains of a cranberry muffin in his stomach. Evidently he ate it just before he died."

"The last muffin," Deedee murmured.

"I beg your pardon?"

"I saw it on the plate before I went to bed," she said. "In the refectory next to the coffee machine. It took a great deal of self-restraint to leave it there, I can tell you. Brother Mortimer's muffins—"

"And what time was that?" the detective said, whipping out his notebook.

"Nine-fifteen, I think. Shortly after the Great Silence began."

"That would have been at nine," he said, consulting a copy of the monastery's brochure.

"Nine, yes."

"Have you talked to Mrs. van Buskirk about what she saw in the night?" Mother Grey asked him. "It might explain the attempt on her life."

"Tell me what you saw," O'Rourke said to the old lady.

She sighed, sat down, crossed her ankles demurely, and took a long breath. "Well, first I got up to go to the bathroom, and—you know the room where we had our retreat discussion with Brother Basil?"

"Upstairs and to the right of the landing," Mother Grey told the detective. "It communicates with the monks' quarters."

"Yes. Well, the door to that opened, and out came two monks, carrying a thing that looked like a coffin between them. The tall one wore a white habit and the short one black."

"We think it was Basil and Christophe," said Mother Grey. "According to Christophe, they carried a chest downstairs and left it in the library. Would you like to see it?"

"I've seen it," said the detective. "Would you happen to know what time this was, Mrs. van Buskirk?"

"I did look at the clock," said Mrs. van Buskirk. "It said eleven minutes after twelve. But, then, I always keep it five minutes fast, so that would be—"

"Six after twelve," said Deedee, making a note in her book.

O'Rourke noticed Deedee's notebook for the first time. "What's that?" he said.

"Mrs. Gilchrist is working out the times," said Mother Grey. "Show him, Deedee."

He took the composition book and looked at it with a deepening frown. "What's all this stuff about Rodman Sedgewick?"

"We think he did it," Deedee said.

"We think he had motive and opportunity," Mother Grey said. "Basil knew something about Sedgewick that he wanted kept quiet. Show him the diary page, Deedee."

Deedee took the sheet of folded paper from her cardigan pocket. "The secret of Rodman Sedgewick's parentage," she said. "Sedgewick tore it out of Basil's diary."

"Where did you get this?" O'Rourke said.

"We stole it from Sedgewick's room," Mother Grey said.

"As you can see from the timetable," Deedee pointed out, "his whereabouts were unknown at the probable time of the murder."

Scowling deeply, he read the paper, reread the schedule in Deedee's notebook, and handed them both back to her. "Unknown to who?"

"His wife," said Mother Grey, realizing even as she said it how it must sound.

"You're kidding, right?" he said. "This has to be some kind of a joke. Ladies, this is a solidly Republican county. I'd have to have a lot more evidence than that before I tried to charge Rodman Sedgewick with murder."

"But what if he attacks someone else?" Mother Grey said.

"If he attacks someone else, call me. If you catch him with the smoking gun in his hand. Do you know how powerful that guy is?"

"No, how powerful is he?" Deedee said.

"Let's just say I can't cross him without a lot more than what I've got. Which is hardly anything." He pulled out a pack of cigarettes and lit up, filling Fergus's chaste office with noxious smoky fumes.

He exhaled through his nose. "For all I know, one of you ladies murdered the monk and cooked up this story to cover it up." Stupefied, they looked at each other and then back at the detective. "Just kidding," he said. "I think."

Fergus tidied up his Liberian photographs and tucked

them into a folder. "Please do what you can for Christophe," he said to O'Rourke. "He's only a boy, and he's suffered so much. If the immigration authorities get him, they'll send him to prison, perhaps for years. He hasn't committed any crime."

"I don't know what I can do," O'Rourke said. "But I do know what needs to be done for this lady. Come on, ma'am, we'll just make a real quick stop at the hospital and let the doctors and nurses take a look at you."

"I don't want to," said Mrs. van Buskirk.

"It'll be good."

She resisted his tug on her arm. "People go into the hospital, and they never come out."

"It'll be all right," the detective insisted. He pulled her gently to her feet.

"Especially elderly people," the old lady said, sitting down again.

"Come on, now." He helped her up again and got her moving forward.

Mother Grey had noticed lately that Mrs. van Buskirk seemed to be having a lot of trouble doing two things at once, such as walking and talking. Nevertheless she managed a few bleats of protest as O'Rourke, still trailing clouds of smoke, propelled her out of Fergus's office. Mother Grey gazed out into the hall as the great oak door to the library swung shut behind them.

O'Rourke's refusal to pursue Sedgewick still annoyed her. "'Do you know how powerful that guy is?'" she mocked.

"No, but if you hum a few bars . . . ," Deedee rejoined. Softly she began to sing: "How powerful that guy is, how powerful—"

"If she were to try again, perhaps your friend the lawyer could get Christophe out now," Fergus said. "Now that there's no reason to suspect him in Basil's death. It isn't right for him to spend even one night in jail."

"Is Martine back?" Deedee said.

"I believe I saw her in the library just now."

Martine was indeed in the library, sitting in the morris chair, laboring over her laptop computer.

"How did it go?" Deedee said.

"Christophe's hearing is tomorrow morning."

"What sort of hearing is it, anyhow? An immigration hearing?"

"It has to do with local procedures. I'm working on it."

"Working on it?" Mother Grey repeated.

"Let's just say that someone I talked to is working on it, and let it go at that. The best thing that could happen is for Christophe never to fall into the hands of the immigration authorities at all, but you didn't hear me say that."

"We're completely deaf," said Deedee. "Did you say something?"

"Somebody tried to smother Delight van Buskirk while you were gone," Mother Grey said.

"Oh, no."

"I'm going to put my things in the car now," said Deedee. "I'm beginning to feel unsafe here, somehow."

"Other things have happened," Mother Grey said.

"Tell me."

Mother Grey glanced around at the bookcases, tall enough to hide a man; the stout chairs, wide enough to conceal a woman; the backs of the nearby guests who were professing to read. She could almost see their ears turning in her direction. "Not here," she said. "Let's go someplace where we can talk. There's something private I want your particular point of view on."

They scurried past the front desk, where Octavian sat poring over the guest register; past the door to the gift shop, where another brother was unpacking a shipment of plaster crucifixes; and out through the front portals. Wet clouds, gray and white, streamed across the blue sky. The air was cool and damp, but there was a smell of spring in it.

The area by the wall where poor Basil's mortal remains had been found was still blocked off with yellow police tape. They walked the other way, only to encounter a crowd of boys from the youth group noisily playing Frisbee. Jonathan Newmont lurked on the sidelines, filming them.

They took still another detour. A quiet path led them around the monastery and down the bank to a huge old tree whose shadow fell across a small boat dock.

A cold wind blew off the river. Mother Grey and Martine leaned against the tree on the leeward side, pulling their collars up.

"This isn't about Mac, is it?" Martine said. "Because I'm sorry I spoke to you the way I did. You have a right to look for your own happiness. What you and Mac do is your business."

"No, no. Forget Mac. This is about Basil's diary. We're trying to figure out whether something he wrote was enough to get him killed. Tell me this. If you were passing for white, and as a result you became rich and famous or whatever, would it be worth doing murder to keep your African ancestry a secret?"

Martine was silent for a long moment, readjusting her thought processes to deal with such a notion. "These days? I don't think so." She looked at her hands, perhaps admiring the perfect brown skin. "Anyway, who would I be trying to fool? The new partners at Sneckman, Flammis? Or who?"

"Make believe you were really white-looking. Make believe a great fortune was at stake, your marriage, maybe your whole life."

"What fortune are you talking about?" Martine was thinking again, mentally surveying all nearby persons of great wealth. "This is about Sedgewick, right?"

"We found a page he tore out of Basil's diary—"

"Rodman Sedgewick, that drooling racist bigot—are you telling me he's a *brother*?"

"A soul brother. Yes. Not a religious brother." Brother Rodman. What an idea. "At least that seemed to be the significance of the diary entry, a reference to interracial marriage between Sedgewick's father and mother."

Martine seemed to find the notion of Sedgewick's African ancestry enormously amusing. When she finished laughing, she sniffed, blew her nose, and declared, "First chance I get, I'm going to out him."

11

"Wait! Wait! Just a minute! I remember!"

A voice rang out from the parking lot, Delight van Buskirk's voice. She and Detective O'Rourke hadn't left yet.

Mother Grey and Martine, heading back to the monastery, detoured from the path, hoping to hear the tale. *She remembers!* They snagged their slacks in the burdocks. When they reached the lot, Mrs. van Buskirk was standing stock still beside a car that must have been the detective's, a dark unmarked late-model four-door sedan, holding her head in her hands, her bag dangling from one elbow.

"Remember what?" the detective said.

"High heels! The second monk was wearing high heels!"

High heels. If it wasn't some dream or fantasy, perhaps this was the very secret to protect which the murderer had tried to silence Mrs. van Buskirk.

"What second monk?" Detective O'Rourke said.

"There were two monks—" Delight van Buskirk began.

The detective acknowledged Mother Grey and Martine with a nod and held up his hand for silence, hoping that Mrs. van Buskirk would find what she meant to remember, but when nothing seemed to be forthcoming, Mother Grey said, "Mrs. van Buskirk told us she saw two monks."

"They were carrying"—the old lady seemed to be rummaging through piles of information in her head, looking for the necessary piece—"carrying—"

"Carrying a coffin," Mother Grey prompted.

"No—yes—oh, I can't remember." The old lady took off her glasses and rubbed her eyes. "What time is it?"

"Two-thirty," Mother Grey said.

"Time to go get checked out," the detective said.

Mrs. van Buskirk felt around in her purse and produced a medicine bottle. "I need a drink of water. I have to take my pill now."

"We'll be there soon," he said. "They have water at the hospital." He half-helped, half-pushed her into the backseat and fastened her seat belt himself. "Fifteen minutes," he said. "I promise."

"I hope you're not going to speed," said the old lady.

He climbed in behind the wheel.

Before he had a chance to close the door, Mother Grey asked him one more question: "Did Basil have anything on his feet when they found him?"

"Sandals," O'Rourke said. "No high heels. I'll see you ladies later." He closed the door, started the car, and was gone, up the hill beyond the parking lot.

Martine shook her head. "High heels?" she said. "How does this fit in with your theory about Rodman Sedgewick?"

"In my heart I know he's guilty," Mother Grey said. "High heels or no."

"I would hate to have you on a jury," Martine said.

The parking lot seemed to be full of vans. When they stepped out from between two of them, they noticed that the wind was rising again. The clouds were lower and thicker, threatening more rain. Martine put the collar of her blazer up; Mother Grey buttoned her sweater; nevertheless it was time to go inside.

In the hall they found Deedee, standing by the refectory door, dripping with coffee. Brother Mortimer was leaving the scene, his mop slung over his shoulder.

"What happened to you?" Mother Grey asked.

"I was attacked," Deedee said. "There's no other word for it. Ouida Sedgewick threw a full mug of coffee all over me, and then under cover of wiping it off, she picked my pocket."

"My word," Mother Grey said.

"What did she take?" Martine asked.

"The page from Basil's diary. Naturally. She knew it had something to do with her."

"Where is she now?"

"She beat it as soon as she found what she was looking for. I think she went to dry it off so she could read it. Guess I'll have to shower and change," she said, examining her stained clothing with dismay.

"I think so," said Mother Grey. Deedee reeked of coffee.

"Means I'll have to take my bags back upstairs and unpack."

"Yep."

"If you see that woman around, give her a snip on the ear for me."

"Will do," said Mother Grey.

"Let's go have coffee," said Martine. "If I'm going to run

into town again to see whether I can get Christophe out, I'll need to get my strength up."

The last gurgle of a fresh batch of coffee trickled into the pot as Mother Grey and Martine entered the empty refectory. Mortimer had cooked another batch of muffins, blueberry this time, light, crumbly, and still warm. The room was as quiet and private as any place they could imagine, so the two women took a table over by the east window, where they sat facing the door.

"So what do you really think?" Martine asked.

"About what?" The coffee was excellent. There really was something about fresh coffee. Maybe she should try making it fresh every time at home, instead of reheating it in the microwave over and over.

"Rodman Sedgewick. Mr. Black America. Much as I hate him, I have a hard time imagining him trying to smother Mrs. van Buskirk," Martine said.

"He'd do it in a heartbeat," Mother Grey said, "and you know it." Mother Grey had a sudden vision of Sedgewick as a twisted Othello figure, Mrs. van Buskirk playing Desdemona. "You've seen him angry, haven't you?"

"Yes, all right, but I can't see him failing. He's a big man, you know. If he wanted to kill that little old lady, it seems like she'd be dead."

"You have a good point." Mother Grey stirred her coffee thoughtfully. "Also, the high heels—"

"If he is the one," said Martine, "he's going to try again. Deedee isn't safe, you and I aren't safe."

"If only there was some way of catching him," Mother Grey said, and let the last crumbs of blueberry muffin disintegrate on her tongue. Then, "Aha. Jonathan Newmont."

"The boy? What about him?" Martine stared. "You think he killed Basil?"

"No, no. But Jonathan has been creeping around the place with a videocamera."

"And so—?"

"What if he caught Sedgewick on tape, murdering Basil?"

"I'm sure he would have mentioned it," Martine said.

"No. I mean, what if we made Sedgewick think Jonathan had caught him on tape? And then what if Sedgewick came to steal the tape back, and a whole bunch of reliable witnesses saw him do this, so that they could testify in court? Wouldn't that force him into a confession?"

"I don't know about a confession," Martine said. "A confession doesn't sound like our Rodman."

"But the witnesses. Surely they would count for something."

"They would all have to be white men," Martine said. "Sedgewick has no fear of anybody else."

"We'll get Fergus and Octavian," Mother Grey said. "Also we'll have to tell Jonathan what we're doing."

"Why?" Martine asked.

"So he can look knowing when knowing looks are called for," Mother Grey said. "And so he can lend us his camera to record whatever happens. A picture is worth a thousand witnesses."

"And if it turns out not to be Sedgewick?"

"Then we'll see who it is."

"This isn't going to put the boy in harm's way, is it?" Martine said. "If the murderer thinks Jonathan photographed him, he would think he saw him do whatever it was he photographed. That would make him the next prospective victim, don't you think?"

"He can hide," Mother Grey said. "As soon as Sedgewick or whoever takes the bait."

Martine drained her coffee. "If you don't mind, Mother Vinnie, I'm going to forget now that we ever had this conversation. Something about your plan feels like getting me disbarred."

"What part would that be?"

"I don't know, but Sedgewick will think of something. I'm going to have another shot at getting Christophe out. If you want me, you can call me at the police station in Vander-vliet."

Mother Grey went to Fergus about it. Fergus thought her plan a little strange, but he agreed to watch with Octavian, and to allow the boy to hide in the monks' quarters, for his own safety, until the trap was sprung.

"When do you want to do this?" he said.

"No time like the present," Mother Grey said. "Give me fifteen minutes. I'll go talk to Jonathan and get set up."

Jonathan was not in the library, although Mother Grey was pleased to note that most of the guests were there, sitting quietly and reading, killing time with their books, awaiting word from the authorities that everyone was free to go home. Sedgewick was among them, not reading actually but sleeping, his morris chair adjusted back to the very last peg-hole, his mouth hanging open. *He'll be there for a while,* she thought. *On with the plan.*

She went upstairs to see whether the boy was in his room. The door was closed, but she could tell someone was in there by the shimmering shape moving behind the glass. She tapped on the door gently.

"Come in," the boy called. She found him changing the battery in his videocamera.

He looked up in a manner guarded and sullen, the typical public demeanor of most of the adolescent boys Mother Grey knew.

"Hi," she said to him.

"Hi." There was a moment of embarrassed silence.

Mother Grey realized she was uncomfortable broaching strange subjects to boys.

At last she plunged in. "I have a job for you, if you want to take it."

"I have to pack," he said. "My sister sent me up here to get my stuff together. We have to leave."

"It could be dangerous," Mother Grey said.

A flicker of interest. "Yeah? What is it?"

Mother Grey sat on the cot next to him. "You know that Brother Basil has been killed," she said.

"It would be hard not to notice," he said.

"We have a plan to trap his killer. But we need your cooperation."

"What do you want me to do?"

"Pretend you made a videotape of the murder."

This seemed to strike the boy as funny; he snickered in an unattractive manner.

"Here's the plan," Mother Grey went on. "I will go down to the library. Everyone will be there. You come in and tell me, loud enough to be overheard, that you made a tape last night around the time of the murder, that you thought it might be evidence, and that you left it in my room."

"Made the tape around the time of the murder, thought it was evidence, left it in your room," he repeated. "That's cool." He smiled broadly. "I like it."

"Can I borrow your camera, also?" Mother Grey asked. "And some tape? I'll pay you for it. Then we can leave the videocamera running in my room and photograph whoever turns up."

"Sure," he said, chuckling. "I can even set it up for you."

"Don't worry about the killer coming after you," she said. "As soon as you make your announcement, you can go and hide in the monks' quarters, where you'll be safe. Brother Mortimer will take care of you."

"What am I gonna do in there?"

"They have TV."

"Cable?"

"I think they have a dish."

"Cool," he said. "Maybe they get MTV. I really miss it out here."

"Oh, and we'll need a dummy tape," Mother Grey said, taking the one on top of the pile. "This one will do nicely, if it's all right with you." The letters RS were scrawled on the label. Even better—that would make Sedgewick think he was on the tape.

"That one?" Jonathan said.

"Any one will do. It isn't as though he—I mean, whoever it is—will be allowed to take it away. The monks will have their eyes on it the whole time." The boy had a strange look on his face. "Is there some problem with using this tape?"

"No," Jonathan said. "It's cool." He laughed. "Cool. But I need to tell my sister what's going on. Okay? She wants us to get going."

"Don't be overheard," Mother Grey said. "And don't tell her the details. Just tell her you're helping us."

"Right," he said.

Ten minutes later all was in readiness. Deedee and Mother Grey found their favorite chairs in the library, within easy eavesdropping distance of Sedgewick, if only the man would wake up. Before she sat down, Mother Grey dragged her chair across the floor with a loud scraping sound. Sedgewick sat up with a snort.

In came Jonathan, exuding a faint odor of ham.

"Mother Grey! I have something to tell you! I made a tape last night around the time of the murder," he declaimed.

"Really!" said Mother Grey.

"I thought it might be evidence," he said, having captured the attention of everyone in the library.

"Where is this tape now?" Deedee prompted.

"I left it in Mother Grey's room," Jonathan said.

"Are you sure? My room is the one that says St. Cuthbert over the door," Mother Grey said.

"St. Cuthbert," the boy said. "Your room. Right. I left it on the bed."

"Thank you," Mother Grey said. "We'll go right up and get it."

It was odd how many people got up and put their books down, making for this or that exit. Father Bingley was the most surprising, but of course his errand was nothing more sinister than a trip to the refectory. Or the bathroom. Which was probably true of the others.

"We'll go up in a minute or two," Deedee said. "Let me just finish this chapter." And so they stalled around, making sure that Sedgewick took the bait.

As presently he did, pushing himself up out of his chair and ambling toward the stairs with a studied air of nonchalance.

"He falls for this stuff every time," Deedee whispered.

What happened next happened so fast that it was all over by the time Mother Grey and Deedee reached the second landing of the guesthouse staircase.

Sedgewick rushed past the head of the stairs in the direction of the men's room. He glanced down and saw them.

"Nice try," he sneered, through the handkerchief he held to his face. "But if you think you can gain some advantage for your friends through acts of extortion, you're very much mistaken. I'll see you in court."

"What is he talking about?" Deedee whispered.

"I guess he thinks we're trying to blackmail him some-how," Mother Grey said.

"But what does he mean, 'I'll see you in court'?"

"Nothing. Lawyers always say that when they feel them-selves at a loss."

Octavian stood in the doorway of the room called St. Cuthbert, bleeding from the nose. Fergus patted his shoulder supportively.

"You guys had a fight?" Deedee said.

"You should have seen *his* nose," Octavian said.

"We did," Deedee said.

"How awful!" Mother Grey said. Octavian nodded, drip-ping on his habit, but she thought she saw behind his hand-kerchief the shadow of a pleased expression.

"You beat him up!" Deedee crowed. "Did you get it all on tape?"

"Come and sit down," Mother Grey said. He sat on the bed. She plucked a handful of fresh tissues from a box on the dresser and gave them to him. "Put your head forward."

"I thought you were supposed to tilt it back," Deedee said.

"Forward," she said. "That's the latest advice. Ice is also good."

"Indeed we got it all on tape," Fergus said. The video-camera was still humming on its perch over the curtain rod. He took it down and turned it off. "This should be a hot item the next time Rodman Sedgewick runs for public office," he said, extracting the tape and slipping the cassette into his clothing somewhere. "A film of Rodman Sedgewick attacking two monks."

"You're not thinking of really blackmailing him?" Mother Grey was horrified. But, wait—how could he run for public office? He would be serving time for the murder of Brother Basil. Wouldn't he?

The flow of blood was slowing. Octavian accepted another handful of clean tissues. Mother Grey thought she heard him chuckling.

"So was that what happened?" Deedee said. "He attacked you?"

"Tell us from the beginning," Mother Grey said.

"From the beginning, Jonathan set up the camera, and the two of us hid behind the curtains," Fergus said.

"Sedgewick didn't notice our feet when he came in," Octavian said. "He gave kind of a shifty look around the room, but it never seemed to occur to him that anyone might be waiting to catch him on purpose, so he didn't poke the curtains or anything."

"What did he do?" Deedee asked.

"He moved straight to the bed and bent over to pick up the cassette," Fergus said.

"So naturally I jumped out to defend it," Octavian said.

"He was mighty surprised," Fergus said.

"Who struck the first blow?" Deedee asked.

"He did, of course," Octavian said. "Please. We are not violent men here." Maybe not. On the other hand, Octavian looked enormously pleased about the whole incident. Mother Grey reflected that even holy monks have testosterone. With his free hand Octavian held up the decoy tape that said RS on the label. "Not violent men. But we aren't weaklings, either. You'll notice he didn't get this tape."

"Octavian," Fergus murmured, shaking his head in reproof.

"It was only a decoy," Mother Grey said.

"You couldn't prove it by the man's behavior. He fought like a tiger."

"Then I stepped out from behind the curtain and remonstrated with him," Fergus said. "Between that and the way his nose was bleeding, he felt that it was time to leave."

"Whew," said Deedee.

The four stood in silence for a while. Octavian dabbed at his nose and seemed to find that the bleeding had stopped. *I have to pack,* Mother Grey thought. *Surely we have enough on Sedgewick now for Detective O'Rourke to arrest him.*

Gradually she realized the other three were staring at the tape Sedgewick had fought for.

"What's really on it?" Deedee said, voicing the thoughts of all.

"Nothing special, I'm sure," Mother Grey said. "Really. I made the whole thing up. That's just some tape that Jonathan had lying around his room with the others. It's only a decoy."

"But what if, by some fantastic coincidence, this tape shows Sedgewick committing the murder?" Deedee said. "What if the story you invented was actually true? What if—"

Fergus took the tape. "We have a VCR in the common room. I can play this and see what's on it."

"Can I see it too?" Deedee asked.

"No, dear," Fergus said. "You aren't allowed into the monks' quarters." Again he slipped the tape into his clothing, and Mother Grey found herself wondering about the pockets in monastic garments. Maybe they were like Japanese kimonos; maybe the monks kept things in their sleeves.

"I'll let you know what shows up on the tape," Fergus said.

"Please do," Mother Grey said. "I'm really curious."

He left softly on his crepe-soled shoes, followed by Octavian. Mother Grey threw some things in her suitcase. Deedee put her head out the door and gazed across the hall at the room called St. Barnabas.

The door was closed.

"Do you suppose Ouida plans to give me back that diary page?" Deedee murmured.

"Is she in there?"

"I think so."

"What's she doing?"

"Digesting the news that Sedgewick's mother was a black person, I guess," Deedee said. "I wonder how she's taking it."

"I don't know Ouida well enough to be able to say," Mother Grey said. "It might not bother her at all."

"They have two children together, don't they?" Deedee said. "Now she has to deal with the fact that they aren't, I don't know, really white."

"Some people would find something like that quite jarring. I just don't know about Ouida."

Jonathan popped in. "How did it go?" he asked. His eyes darted around the room, then went to the bed. The tape marked RS was not where he had left it.

"It went very well," Mother Grey said. "Here's your camera. Let us pay you for the tapes." She took out her wallet.

"Can I have that one tape back?" he said.

"The one we were using for a decoy?"

"Yeah."

"What's on it?" Deedee said.

"Nothing. Some stuff," he said. "It cost me five ninety-eight. There's nothing on it that you want. I need to pack it now. My sister wants to go home."

"I'm sorry," Mother Grey said, "Brother Fergus must still have it. I'll get it for you." The boy gnawed his lip.

What's really on that tape? The question was becoming more and more interesting.

12

Nobody was in the library when Mother Grey and Deedee went there to keep a vigil for news of the Fatal Tape. From time to time someone went past carrying luggage toward the front door, or carrying an empty mug back to the refectory. The two women sat in silence, twiddling their thumbs.

Ouida appeared from the direction of the refectory with a plate of coconut cookies. "Mortimer just baked these," she said. "He always cooks when he's upset." They smelled wonderful. "I read the diary page that you found in Rodman's pants," she added.

"I thought you might," Deedee said.

"Why didn't you want me to see it?" Ouida said. "You were, what, protecting me? You thought it would bother me?"

"Yes," Mother Grey said.

"Well, it doesn't bother me. I don't give a rat's patoot who or what Rodman's mother was. The thing that bothers me is that he didn't tell me."

Deedee said, "He never told you?"

"No," Ouida said. "But he's my man. I love him. Why would he think I cared?" She held out the plate of cookies. "Have an octoroon. I mean a macaroon. Oh, God," she said.

It really wasn't that funny, rather tasteless in fact (not like the cookies), but the three of them started laughing hysterically just the same.

Rodman Sedgewick appeared. "What's so funny?"

Ouida pulled the diary page out of her pocket and held it out to him.

He looked at it without touching it, looked at his wife, and looked back at the paper. His face reddened and swelled perceptibly. Mother Grey had never seen the man caught in a bit of deception, but this was apparently how he reacted.

"I was going to tell you," he said.

Ouida gave the page to Deedee. "We need to talk, Rodman," she said.

"It's a bad time," he said. "A bad time. I don't need this right now." He turned his back on her and strode toward the stairs.

She followed him. "All the same," she said. They went up to their room, or Mother Grey supposed that was where they went; maybe Sedgewick went into the men's room. Mother Grey imagined him barricading himself in a stall, Ouida marching in after him, pounding on the door. *Come out, you coward.*

Deedee said, "He was going to tell her, he says. I wonder when. They've been married for—what? twenty or thirty years?"

"Sedgewick's flaws have nothing to do with his ancestry, and everything to do with the sort of person he just naturally is. I'm sure Ouida knows this perfectly well," Mother Grey said.

"But he could still have wanted to keep it from her."

"True."

"Wanted it badly enough to silence Brother Basil."

"Too, too true." Mother Grey sighed a long sigh and ran her fingers through her hair. "We never got a chance to ask Delight about the black monks," she said. "The ones with the throne. Remember that one?"

"We'll talk to her when she comes back," Deedee said. "I'm sure it was nothing but a dream."

"I'm not so certain," said Mother Grey. "What if—?" Monks in high heels? She closed her eyes, and across her mental field of vision pranced a long line of multicolored monks, shod in ridiculous footgear of many sorts, holding hands, carrying chests, carrying thrones.

"Did you see his face?" Deedee said. "He puffed up."

Sedgewick. The wretch was still worth talking about, if only for his entertainment value. "There was definitely some swelling involved," Mother Grey agreed. They thought about him puffing up until they started laughing again. Deedee lost control of herself completely; Mother Grey thought her friend was going to slide right into a bout of weeping.

"Are you okay?"

"I'm a little tense," Deedee said.

"Basil's death has been a strain on everyone," Mother Grey said.

"It isn't even that. Why do you think I was so anxious to bring you all here this weekend? I needed to get away from Holy Assumption."

"Any reason in particular?" she asked. "Or life in general?"

"My career in the Church," Deedee said. "Canon Spelving doesn't seem very interested in advancing it."

"He won't give you a recommendation," Mother Grey guessed. Deedee was serving an apprenticeship with the Reverend Canon Arthur Spelving at Holy Assumption in Ocean Prospect; without his okay, Deedee would never be ordained as a priest in the Diocese of New Jersey.

"Not this year."

"Does he give any reason?"

"I couldn't make it out; something about not having what it takes. It sounded as though he were accusing me of lack of maturity. I'm older than he is, you know."

"Maybe you should try to be more, I don't know, pompous."

"I yam what I yam," Deedee said.

They sat in silence for a while, brooding upon Church politics, when an old and perplexing question floated into Mother Grey's mind. "Deedee," she asked, "why is Canon Spelving's church called Holy Assumption?"

"What?"

"Why do they call your church Holy Assumption? I've been wondering about that for a long time. It's such a strange name for an Episcopal church. The doctrine of the Holy Assumption is Roman, and very recent at that. It dates from the early fifties, doesn't it? Pope Pius?"

"Ah. Right. The doctrine that the Virgin Mary never died but was assumed bodily into Heaven. But Holy Assumption in Ocean Prospect used to be a Roman church. Didn't you know that?"

"How can this be?"

"It's a holy mystery."

"No, really."

So Deedee launched into the gripping story of how the entire parish of Holy Assumption managed to wander away from the Roman fold and into the camp of the Anglo-Catholics. Mother Grey ran her fingers idly over the chair arm, listening with moderate interest as her friend developed each amazing plot twist. It all started with Vatican II, Deedee explained, and went more or less downhill from there.

As Deedee described the tidal wave of ecumenism that washed over Ocean Prospect, New Jersey, in 1966—"Ecumenical tsunami," she said, "it sounds like a good name for a movie"—Mother Grey thought idly, *Where is the dent in the wood that Martine put here yesterday?* The chair arm was perfectly smooth.

By the time Deedee reached the point in the tale where Father O'Hallahan proposed marriage to Sister Mary Theresa, Mother Grey suddenly saw the answer to the riddle of the chair arm.

"Two little blackbirds sitting on a hill," she muttered. "One named Jack, the other named Jill. Fly away, Jack! Fly away, Jill! Come back, Jack! Come back, Jill!"

"I must say, Vinnie, you're getting to be as dotty as poor old Delight van Buskirk. She's the one who's supposed to be reciting nursery rhymes. Your role is to be wise and sober."

"I was just reminded of that nursery rhyme. It was a game my grandmother used to play when I was little, with bits of paper stuck to her fingers. She would recite the rhyme and put up different fingers so that it looked as though the bits of paper disappeared and then reappeared miraculously. As I remember, it was her best magic trick."

"Is there a point to all this?"

"Oh, yes. The point is that this chair is like Granny's finger. The dent that Martine put on the arm is gone, and the reason is that this isn't the same chair that was here yesterday. Look here."

They examined it carefully. Mother Grey looked with particularly keen attention at the inlay on the central splat that had so charmed her when first she saw the chair. It was similar, but the design was slightly different, and in fact it was a clever decal, not real inlay at all.

13

Father Bingley and Martha sat on a log overlooking the Hudson River, holding hands.

"You're upset, Rupert," Martha said. "What is it?"

"Nothing," he said. "I don't know. Intimations of mortality."

"Are you afraid of being murdered too? Poor Basil, such a sweet old dear. I can't imagine anyone wanting to do him harm."

"No, no. I'm afraid of being—I'm afraid of being ineffectual." This was something he would never have confessed to another living soul, not even his bishop, but he could trust Martha not to take it amiss.

"You're still thinking of that little black monk, aren't you?" she said.

"There are so many things to do, so many things," he said. "Sometimes I'm not sure I'm doing the right ones."

"There, there," she said, and patted his hand. "You're just tired."

"Yes," he said. He continued to stare out over the water; the rising wind was making ripples on it; to the north he thought he could see a spatter of rain. "But now it's time to get back to Rolling Hills, my dear."

"Did you put everything in the car?" she asked.

"All but my briefcase," he said. "Let's go say good-bye to Fergus and Octavian."

"The weekend was very nice," Martha said. "Except for poor, poor Brother Basil. I only wish—" But what she wished for, Father Bingley was never to hear.

He was hit on the head with a rock.

Well, all right, not quite a rock, more of a small stone. Someone on the bank above was flinging little flat stones at the water. One was badly aimed and clipped Father Bingley on his balding crown, making it bleed.

Grinding his teeth, Father Bingley charged up the path and around the corner, only to find Jonathan Newmont with his arm cocked back for another throw. "Stop that!" he said. "There are people below on that path! If you must skip stones, go down to the water and do it."

"Oh. Sorry, Father," said the youth. He put the stones in his pocket and went skulking down the trail.

As soon as he was out of sight, Father Bingley remembered opening the door of the boy's room the night before and finding it empty. Except for a fog of marijuana smoke.

Martha came up the path toward him. "Are you all right, Rupert?"

"That boy is troubled," Father Bingley said.

"Your head is cut. Let me see to it," she said.

"Last night I told myself I would speak to him. He was

gone from his room when I got up in the night, and his room was all full of smoke."

"I think we should wash this cut. He was smoking in his room?"

"Yes, and not tobacco."

"You don't mean drugs, Rupert."

"I do."

"Oh, dear." She sighed. "So many temptations for a young person nowadays. You'll try to help him, of course."

"Of course," he said. But how? When he was in seminary, the last thing they expected to have to deal with was drug abuse; Trinitarian theology and managing a church budget—that's what they talked about, or at least that's what he remembered. It was all a long time ago. Now every seminary graduate had taken at least one course in substance abuse counseling.

"I know you're equal to the challenge," Martha said. "The Lord will support you in your efforts."

"As He always has," Father Bingley said. But drug abuse counseling. What do you say to them?

As they made their way back to the monastery, Martha took his hand again and squeezed it gently.

"There is some deep plot here," Mother Grey said. The library darkened suddenly, as though some malign spirit had come to fill it up. It was probably a cloud passing across the sun, or the sun sinking behind the evergreen hedge. The afternoon was drawing in.

"A plot, yes," Deedee said. "But what?"

"Fake furniture is being substituted for real furniture," Mother Grey said.

"You don't mean the brothers are selling off their antique mission furniture?"

"Something like that," said Mother Grey.

"To whom?"

"Interesting question."

"And where are they getting these fakes?"

Mother Grey thought of stained fingers, little trails of hardwood sawdust. "Octavian's workshop, would be my guess," she said.

"Let's go talk to Octavian, then," said Deedee.

They found him manning the guest desk.

Octavian was speaking to someone on the phone. "I'm sorry, the guesthouse is full next weekend," he said. "The weekend after that we have six vacancies. . . . Yes. . . . Thank you." He hung up, wrote something down in the guest book, and looked up at them, smiling, a lock of straight sandy hair falling into his ocean-blue eyes. "What can I do for you ladies?"

"Tell us about your work," Mother Grey said.

"As guestmaster?"

"As furniture maker. I have an absorbing interest to know what you mean by honest furniture."

He looked from one to another of their grim faces and sighed. "The easiest thing would be for you to see the workshop," he said. "If you'll come with me, I'll show you. There's an outside entrance so that we won't have to go through the cloistered quarters." He turned on the answering machine and abandoned the desk.

A damp chill had settled over the little knoll where the monastery perched among its seedy muddy lawns. Mother Grey shivered. Octavian led them around yellow plastic crime scene tape to get to the workshop entrance. It was beyond the iron gate that led to the garden where they had first met Christophe, beyond the shed roof where the wood was stacked to season and dry. Big double doors, chained and padlocked, opened to Octavian's key.

"Here it is," he said, with more pride than Mother Grey

would have thought seemly in a cloistered monk. But his pride was justified. The workshop was wonderful.

Over the great workbench with its array of businesslike vises were racks of tools: hand tools, machine tools, clamps of every size and shape, glass jars of screws, blades, and bits, each in its perfect place. Those parts of the plain board walls not covered with shelves or closed cupboards were papered with plans, neatly arranged. Brilliant lighting illuminated large machine tools, benches, sawhorses, and work in various stages of completion.

A dehumidifier hummed softly. Octavian shut the door to keep the carefully controlled air in. The smells were bracing: hardwood sawdust, turpentine, hide glue. It was enough to make a woman want to take up woodworking.

Next to some partially finished pieces in one corner, there were carefully arranged piles of wood of many colors. Mother Grey recognized oak and cherry and put out her hand to touch a piece of very dark, close-grained wood on top of a stack.

"That's ebony," Octavian said. "Basil brought it from Africa. We use it for inlay."

Against the far wall of the workshop stood an oak table and three straight chairs. The chairs lacked only the customary rush seats and dark finish. A fourth was up on sawhorses. The sight of these pieces revealed at last to Mother Grey what Octavian meant by "honest furniture." He meant the sort of stuff that graced the monastery library: Arts and Crafts style mission oak.

If honesty meant diligence and care in the making, then these chairs that Octavian was working on were very honest indeed. But if honesty meant making a plain statement of what you were all about, then it might be that they were just the tiniest bit deceitful. Because the table they were being made to match could have passed for a hundred-year-old antique.

Well, maybe it was. "Is this old?" said Mother Grey.

"About a week old," Octavian said. "Christophe finished distressing it last week. For my taste, it could stand one more going over with steel wool and polish."

"Distressed it?" Mother Grey asked.

"Beat on it."

"With what?" Deedee said.

"A hide hammer, a sack of pebbles, barbed wire wrapped around a stick. Seemed to enjoy himself." He picked up a leathery hammer and gave one of the chairs a whack. "We all do it sometimes to relieve tension. Would you like a try?"

"Perhaps later," Deedee said. "Do you darken your things with ammonia, the way the Stickleys did?"

"No. Nowadays we achieve that effect with a water-based aniline stain," Octavian said.

"What did they use to do with ammonia?" asked Mother Grey.

"Ammonia fumes darkened the oak," Octavian said. "The sanded pieces were put in an airtight chamber with dishes of ammonia and left for a week or so. It showed the grain to a nice advantage, especially on quarter-sawn boards. If I tried to set up an ammonia chamber now, I'm afraid I'd get a hard time from the Environmental Protection Agency. Anyway the aniline dyes are easier to control."

"That's why these chairs are all blond," Deedee said. "You haven't done them yet."

"Not yet," he said. "Christophe was going to stain them before he rushed the seats. He's getting quite good at rushing seats. His work is better than mine." He picked up what seemed to be a chair part and began to sand it, almost idly, running a sandpaper-wrapped block the length of the grain and back. As he bent over his work, his hair almost hid his eyes. "I hope they let him return here. Have you heard anything?"

"They're holding him overnight at the jail in Vandervliet. There's some sort of hearing tomorrow morning," Deedee said.

"But I thought, since there had been another attack after they arrested him—"

"The immigration authorities want to deal with him in some way," Mother Grey said. "You knew he was in this country illegally, didn't you?"

"Was he," said Octavian. "I guess I never thought to ask for his papers. He's been so helpful here in the shop. There's so much work."

"None of the other brothers work with you?" Mother Grey asked.

"Sometimes they give me a hand, as much as they're capable of, but Christophe has a gift. Surprising, really, when you consider the sort of environment he came from. His people don't think of wood as an art material, you know. To them it's something they use to boil their water and cook their food, when they can get it."

"You mean tribal Africans don't work in wood?" Mother Grey said.

"Oh, yes," said Octavian. "They do marvelous things. But the material is so ephemeral."

"Ephemeral?"

"It's the climate. It rots everything. I've seen tribal masks only a few years old nearly destroyed by insects."

Yet another reason why Mother Grey had never felt called to do missionary work in Africa. Shots, horrible diseases, intertribal strife, and now dampness and bugs.

"Sounds almost like Fishersville," Deedee said.

"It's true that the rectory is damp," Mother Grey said. "I

remember one summer I left a pair of shoes on the closet floor, and when I went to get them—"

"Since when have you got an extra pair of shoes?" Deedee said.

"Well, they were winter shoes. But I never did get all the mold off." She picked up a small table with an inlaid design. "This is lovely."

"It is, isn't it?" Octavian said. "Christophe did that. Something new we're trying, African art without the termites."

"So," Mother Grey said, "I thought the style was slightly different from your . . . reproductions."

"You do everything by hand?" Deedee asked.

"Not at all. With just the two of us in here, we need all the technological help we can get. For instance, I'm all set to smooth this with a hand-held belt sander. I'll show you. You might want to step back," he said. "There's going to be dust." He slipped a mask over his nose and mouth and turned on the sander. With surprising delicacy he applied it to a flat piece of oak secured to the workbench by clamps. It made a terrible noise.

Conversation was impossible, so Mother Grey found her mind wandering, gnawing at the problem of exactly what it was that was going on in this workshop. Something was coming back to her, something she had seen long ago in one of the old copies of *Yankee* magazine that Granny kept at the summer camp. It had to do with a hoax perpetrated by a craftsman, who had taken it into his head to counterfeit a Great Brewster, a famous chair of the sort that came over on the *Mayflower*.

The craftsman made the chair with great care and patience, the way Octavian was making these. It took him months; he began with a tree in his own backyard, cured and dried the wood—not too much, what he wanted was an old, warped look—put the chair together, painted it, took most of the paint off again, ripped out the front rung. When he had the chair looking ancient and somewhat ill-used, he planted it beside the hearth in his little New England home and invited a greedy antique dealer he knew to supper.

The dealer fell for it, so the story went; he offered the craftsman money—probably about what the work was worth, though considerably less than the going rate for a Great Brewster—and with an air of carelessness the craftsman sold it to him. After passing through a number of hands the chair wound up in a museum of early American furniture.

How easy it would be to do that here. Make a good fake Stickley, put it in the library, invite a dealer, put up a false show of reluctance, and then sell it to him for an original antique.

Octavian turned off the sander.

"So this is your bold and forward-looking plan for financing St. Hugh's," Mother Grey said.

"I think it will help, yes," he said, brushing the sawdust off the sanded oak splat.

"What did Basil think of your plan?"

"Nothing. Why should he think anything of it?"

"A racket to counterfeit antiques?" Mother Grey said.

"I'm not counterfeiting antiques, Mother Grey, I'm making handcrafted reproductions. This is not a racket."

"You must confess, Brother Octavian, that it seems a little outré," Deedee said.

"I can see that I'm going to have to tell you the whole story," he said.

"Go ahead. We're all ears."

"All right. It begins," he said, "with the death of Minerva Ellis Wackerby."

* * *

In the refectory Father Bingley consoled himself for the wound on his head by devouring the second-to-last blueberry muffin. Resting on a stool by the side of the coffee counter, pinching the last crumbs from the palm of his left hand—how the moist crumbs clung together!—he considered whether to eat the very last muffin as well.

No one would care. And who was to know? It wasn't as though people were swarming into the refectory demanding muffins. The smooth, sweet, almost crisp, slightly buttery crust, the tender crumb of the inside parts, the surprising yet delightful jolt of the sour blueberries—fresh blueberries, too, not canned or frozen. Where could Mortimer have obtained fresh blueberries at this time of year? It would be three or four months before fresh blueberries were obtainable in New Jersey, and probably longer than that before Father Bingley could get his lips around another such muffin.

Unless he took this one.

And as he had pointed out to himself, no one would care; no one was here.

There was a rush of air as the refectory door swung open. Swift as a pouncing cat, Father Bingley's hand darted out and secured the muffin, almost, he would have said, without his volition.

A woman spoke, in a voice that was high and almost whispering with agitation: "What do you mean, you didn't get it?"

"The monks have still got it," Rodman Sedgewick said. "I couldn't get it away from them. They were guarding it. One of them hit me in the face. It was the damnedest thing."

Got what? For a moment he thought they meant the muffin, and he quickly stuffed it in his pocket. They didn't seem to realize he was there. Evidently they couldn't see him. He could see them, though; at least he could see their knees, though the cupboard hid their faces. Odd that a woman would wear her skirts so short in a monastery.

"Do they know what's on it?" she said.

Father Bingley drew in his breath, preparing to clear his throat loudly and make himself known, since they were evidently speaking of something private.

Sedgewick said, "How would they know what's on it? They're monks. They wouldn't have anything to play it on."

"They have something to play it on. There's a VCR in the monks' quarters," she said.

"I see," he said, and there was something so menacing about his tone of voice that Father Bingley jumped to his feet at once to forestall a possible violent act.

Sedgewick was startled. "Ah, Father," he said. "Good afternoon."

"How are you, Rodman?" said Father Bingley. "Miss Newmont." What a fluffy creature, with her twinkling knees and her long yellow hair. Sedgewick did not appear to be threatening her. *It must have been my imagination.* "I was just leaving. Excuse me." Embarrassed by his own odd perceptions, Father Bingley moved toward the door, brushing muffin crumbs from his vest.

Beryl Newmont clattered the coffeepot and mugs. "There's only one cup left," she said to Sedgewick. "Do you want it, or do you want to wait while I make a fresh pot?"

"I'll take it," Sedgewick said, and grabbed it out of her hand without thanking her. On his way out the door, muttering to himself, "What a mess," he jostled Father Bingley, who was to discover later that Sedgewick had elbowed the muffin in his jacket pocket, reducing it to crumbs and stains.

In the shop Octavian continued the tale of Minerva Ellis Wackerby. "She was a devout Episcopalian," he explained, "and came frequently to St. Hugh's on retreat. All her sons attended the school that used to be here. When she went to her reward and the will was read, it was discovered that she had left the contents of her house to the monastery."

"I had heard the story of her legacy," Deedee said, "but I had forgotten her name."

"Mrs. Wackerby collected French antiques. Most of the furniture was sold for a very nice figure," Octavian said. "The new refectory was built from the proceeds of that sale. But then, in her attic, they found more than a dozen old oak pieces in the Arts and Crafts style. They were out of fashion at the time. The man who was then prior decided the monastery could make more use of them as furniture than by trying to sell them. Very sturdy things, made to last forever. I find them beautiful, and of course in the last thirty years public taste has come back around to agree with me."

"You mean they're worth a lot of money now?" said Deedee.

"Yes. But by now they're part of what makes St. Hugh's what it is. We would sell them only as a last resort."

"So you decided to copy them," Mother Grey prompted.

"It was an exercise at first," he said. "Just to see if I could do it."

"How long have you been doing this sort of thing?" Mother Grey asked.

"I've always worked in wood. My father had a wonderful workshop. I grew up with it. When I came here ten years ago to join the order, the Minerva Ellis Wackerby collection was here already; the style was starting to come back into fashion; I got to thinking maybe I could make reproductions to raise money for the order."

"Can you just look at a piece of furniture and figure out how to reproduce it?" Deedee asked.

"Some people can," he said. "I can't. I need plans. It's always helpful to have the piece in front of you, but there are plans available for making many of Gustave Stickley's designs. I found them in reprints of the old *Craftsman* magazine. It hasn't been difficult. A lot of work, but not difficult."

"Counterfeit Stickleys," said Deedee.

"Of course you would want to keep this hushed up," said Mother Grey.

He looked from one to the other of them, realizing at last what they were leading up to, a motive for Basil's murder. "You think I—"

"It had crossed our minds," Deedee said.

A saber saw lay near at hand. He picked it up, and for a horrible instant Mother Grey thought, *He knows we know, and now he's going to kill us.* It wasn't plugged in, though, and instead of looking around for an outlet *(surely we can run farther than the length of the cord, before he gets us!),* Octavian opened a cardboard box that had been underneath the saw.

"The furniture business at St. Hugh's is completely aboveboard," he said. "We have no need to hide it. On the contrary, we advertise it." He reached into the cardboard box and came out with a stack of two-color glossy pamphlets. "We sell our work as handcrafted reproductions, not original antiques. We get a lot of business from decorators. Here's the latest brochure."

"Benedictine Mission Reproductions," it said, with photos of a few samples on the front and a picture of Octavian at work in his long white habit.

It was an attractive presentation. "Did you design this too?" Deedee asked.

"No, no. I'm not much of a graphic artist. Mortimer did those. When we get the equipment, we're going to work up a home page on the World Wide Web." He brushed his fore-lock back off his face. "I can't believe you thought—"

"Did you ever have a failure?" Mother Grey asked.

"What do you mean?"

"When you were getting started at this, did you ever make a reproduction so clumsy that you couldn't offer it for sale?"

"I hope I may be excused of the sin of pride if I say that I haven't done anything particularly clumsy since I was eleven. In the way of joinery, at any rate."

"I was thinking of the little chair in the library with the leaves on the back," Mother Grey said.

"That was made by Harvey Ellis himself in the old Crafts-man workshop of Gustave Stickley," said Octavian. "He was Minerva's father. It's a masterpiece, one of a kind. I'd hardly call it clumsy."

"It was replaced sometime last night with a mediocre re-production. I take it this was not one of your early efforts."

"Replaced! You must be mistaken."

"I don't think so."

"That chair is priceless." He put down the saw and sprang to his feet. "Replaced! It can't be. Are you sure?"

"Come and see," said Mother Grey.

The last ray of afternoon sun peeped between two ever-greens and through the far window of the guesthouse li-brary, where it slanted along the terracotta tile floor and struck the fake chair like the accusing finger of God.

"There it is," said Mother Grey. "See for yourself."

Octavian rushed to the little chair and began to handle it, turning it this way and that. As he did this, there came a bumping sound from the stairway. Mother Grey turned to see Ouida Sedgewick coming down, dragging her black wheeled airline bag behind her.

She wore a little smile, and her cheeks were pink. As she reached the bottom of the stairs, Sedgewick charged across the library carrying a sloshing mug of coffee.

They met. Her hand on his arm, Ouida lifted her face to be kissed, a sweet married peck. So they were on good terms now. Whatever had passed between them when Ouida cornered Sedgewick in the upstairs parts for a talk, the outcome had apparently been satisfactory, to Ouida at least. *Imagine being in love with Rodman Sedgewick*, Mother Grey thought. *What horror.*

"Give me a minute to finish this coffee, and I'll take your suitcase out," Sedgewick said. He tasted the coffee. "Ugh! it's cold," he said.

"It's still steaming," his wife said. "You drink it too hot, Roddy. You're going to ruin your stomach one day."

"Here, then. You drink it."

"Thank you," she said. She took the coffee and gave him another kiss. He took the suitcase and towed it toward the front door.

Octavian, meanwhile, was on his knees in front of the Harvey Ellis chair, running his hands over the backsplat, tilting it and looking underneath. "Incredible," he muttered. "Incredibly bad work. See how the glue runs down in drips."

"Do you still want me to mind the gift shop this afternoon?" Ouida asked him.

"What?" Octavian said.

She drained the last dregs of the coffee. "I was scheduled for gift shop duty from four to five."

"Oh, yes. Yes, please, Mrs. Sedgewick."

"I'll just gather up these mugs first and take them to the refectory." They could hear her progress, clinking and clattering as she puttered around the library collecting the dirty dishes.

"So what's the story?" Deedee asked. "Is it a fake?"

"A fake," Octavian said, "and a very bad one. I'm going to have to report this to the police. Does it have something to do with Basil's death, do you think?"

Deedee produced the diary page and read:

"'The arthritis is worse and worse, and I find myself thinking that if I only had a good chair in here instead of this hard chest, I could continue my studies for much longer at a stretch.'"

"This suggests that Basil brought the chest downstairs to make room in his cell for a chair," Mother Grey said.

"It almost looks that way, doesn't it?" Octavian said, stroking his chin.

"So it must have been when Basil went to take the chair to his room that the murderer—"

"But where is the real Harvey Ellis chair?" Mother Grey asked. "Nobody has left the parking lot since last night."

"Except Martine," said Deedee.

Oh, for Heaven's sake. "Octavian, do the monks keep track of the cars in the guesthouse parking lot?"

"Yes indeed. During the hunting season we have a problem with unauthorized people parking in our lot, and so we have procedures. To park in the lot, you have to be in the register."

"May we see the register?" Deedee asked.

"Certainly." He led them out to the registration desk and flipped open the big brown book. "Parking . . . here we are. Chris Williams, leading the youth hostel party from Berkeley, California, one bus. A very pleasant young woman."

"I thought the youths were all on bicycles," Deedee said. Mother Grey found herself imagining pleasant young women from Berkeley, California, carrying away the monastery's chairs, hiding them in the back of the bus.

"The riders are accompanied by the bus for support, in case of excessive fatigue, medical emergency, mechanical breakdown, or whatever. California is a long way off."

"I see. And what else is there?"

"Father Bingley's party, two vehicles."

"What vehicles?"

"A black Mercedes-Benz—that would be Rodman Sedgewick's car—and a brown Dodge van belonging to Miss Newmont."

"We'll go and look," said Mother Grey, but as they headed for the door, another terrific crash of crockery sounded, in the library this time.

"Sedgewick again," Deedee muttered. "Now what is he trying to distract our attention from?"

As they filed back into the library to see what was up, Brother Mortimer went rushing past with his broom. They assumed the good monk had everything under control until they heard him speak, long and low, almost in a moan: "Ooooh, *my.*"

It must be more than dishes this time, thought Mother Grey. It was. On the floor behind the bookcase lay Ouida Sedgewick, the broken pieces of many cups strewn around her unconscious form.

14

"What happened?" Deedee said. Ouida Sedgewick lay curled at their feet, her breathing shallow, her eyes rolled back, her skin pale and cold to the touch.

Octavian said, "I can't imagine. Heart attack? Stroke? A fit of some kind?"

"Could be that. She's certainly been under a strain," Deedee said. They put a cushion under her head and loosened her clothes. She made not the slightest response.

"She might have been poisoned," Mother Grey said. "Which of these fragments came from her cup?"

"You mean that cup of coffee Sedgewick gave her?" Deedee said.

"No matter," Octavian said. "We'll leave that to the police. Let me go call them and get an ambulance." He rushed away to the telephone.

"Should we sit her up and try to make her vomit?" Mother Grey asked.

"Not while she's unconscious," Deedee said. "I think we're supposed to keep her head lower than her heart."

Footsteps approached, and Sedgewick appeared between the bookcases, blocking the light. Water dripped from his hair. It must be raining again.

"My God! What have you done to my wife?"

"What have you done to your own wife?" Mother Grey said. He crouched down beside Ouida, felt her face, brushed the hair from her eyes.

"Wouldn't you think there would be a first aid book here someplace?" Deedee said, poking through the stacks. "Here's a prayer book, though. Do you think it's time for the last rites? What did you give her, Roddy?"

A beat of silence while Sedgewick grasped her question. "I gave her a cup of lukewarm coffee! What's the matter with you women!" He chafed his wife's hands and murmured her name: "Ouida, Ouida." She moaned and twitched but did not regain consciousness.

"Sit her up, and we'll tickle the back of her throat," Deedee offered.

"Get away from her," Sedgewick said.

"If you think we're going to leave you alone with her so you can finish the job, forget it," Deedee said.

Sedgewick growled with rage: "Aaargh!" Mother Grey thought for a moment that he was going to jump up and go for Deedee's throat.

Octavian returned then. "They're on their way," he said. He and Sedgewick exchanged a look, but they did not offer to punch each other again. Other people began to wander in also; one by one nearly everyone in the monastery came and crowded around poor Ouida, so that Mother Grey found herself asking them to stand back and give her air.

How corny. But then, it was all so corny. Brother Mortimer clutching his broom and dustpan. Beryl and Jonathan Newmont, gazing soberly. The Smartts, holding hands and biting their lips (their own lips, that is, not each other's, Mother Grey was relieved to see). Martha and Rupert Bingley.

"How is she?" Father Bingley said. "Do you think—?" Mother Grey had a feeling he was trying to offer the last rites, but Sedgewick shot him a baleful look and he subsided.

Sedgewick, the miserable hypocrite, was putting on such an act of husbandly devotion that Mother Grey thought she would throw up herself if they couldn't get Ouida to do it soon. With her own eyes she had seen him poison the woman. (It was poison, wasn't it? Yes, certainly. Everything added up. She and Deedee both had seen him hand her the cup, using the ploy of claiming it was too cold.) The cunning wretch. No inner core of self, none whatsoever.

Outside they heard the roar and rush of the medevac helicopter landing in the monastery parking lot. Sedgewick picked up his wife, letting her arms hang limply, and carried her outdoors to meet the medics.

Frankenstein's monster, Mother Grey thought.

"Watch him," Deedee whispered. They dogged his footsteps, certain that he would try to wring her neck or smother her as soon as everyone was out of sight. In a moment the medics appeared, trundling a gurney up the stone walk, the wheels bumping. Coolly they took charge.

As Sedgewick placed Ouida on the gurney—tenderly, Mother Grey would have said, if she didn't know better— the noise reached another crescendo, as the police came howling over the hill in their black-and-whites. Detective O'Rourke popped out of the first car. A number of minions gathered around him, and he directed their efforts here and there. He did not seem pleased.

"Detective O'Rourke!" Deedee called. "We saw it all! We'll tell you everything."

And so they got him behind the police car and told him everything, how Ouida Sedgewick had come to discover that her husband of twenty-five years had been deceiving her about his background, how their money was all hers, how he had fought two burly monks for a videotape under the impression that it showed his activities on the night of Basil's murder, how they had seen him hand his rich wife a cup of coffee, how they had seen her drink it, how she had collapsed almost at once.

Later Mother Grey thought, *I forgot to mention the Harvey Ellis chair.* But that was then.

By the time the medics had loaded Ouida Sedgewick into the helicopter and prepared for takeoff, Mother Grey and Deedee had managed to finger Rodman Sedgewick as thoroughly as the job could be done.

"Lady detectives," O'Rourke growled.

Nevertheless their testimony was enough to cause him to take official action. Sedgewick had one foot in the helicopter when O'Rourke and his men grabbed him by the arms.

"Excuse me, sir. You're under arrest."

"Under arrest for what?" Sedgewick said.

"For the attempted murder of your wife. These ladies will testify that they saw you poison her."

Sedgewick didn't go "Aaargh" quite so loud with a couple of sturdy policemen hanging on his arms, but Mother Grey and Deedee knew he was thinking it all right, the way he looked at them. It was all Mother Grey could do to keep from smirking as they put the handcuffs on him, restraining the very hands he had laid so violently on her the other time, the time with the polo mallet. After that incident nothing bad had happened to him, no retribution whatever other than the fate of living with his own poisonous personality; she hadn't pressed charges or even told anyone except Deedee. *But the mills of justice grind exceeding small,* she told herself. As she savored her moment of triumph, Martine drove up and parked the minivan. Delight van Buskirk was in the passenger seat. Mother Grey was pleased to note, when the old lady alighted, that she carried a new plastic sack labeled "Mary's Yarn Shoppe." Now she would have two needles. Maybe three.

Ouida's helicopter took off straight up. In the whirlwind of leaves and twigs, Officers Timmerman and Case tried to stuff Sedgewick into the police car.

"I never prepared that coffee," Sedgewick claimed. "That coffee came from Beryl Newmont. She fixed it and then gave it to me, probably with the intention of poisoning me."

"Watch your head, sir," said Officer Case.

He banged it anyway; the bump made him mad enough to start raving. "I'll have your job! I'll sue you for false arrest!" Before the policemen could close the door, he put his head out for a parting shot at Mother Grey and Deedee. "If my wife dies without me at her side, I'll sue you women for everything you ever had or ever will have!" His face was a worse color this time than on the day he had swung at her with the polo mallet, darker red, with a little touch of blue now.

"Go for it," Deedee sneered, as the police car carried him away. "The joke's on you. I never had anything and never will."

"All the same," Mother Grey said, "I hope Ouida pulls through. For one thing, I was just beginning to like her."

15

But the chair. Where was it? Mother Grey resolved to make a cursory search of the vehicles in this parking lot. She tried to think of the chair, estimate its size, but it was now a phantom chair, being out of her reach for touching purposes; like anything stolen or lost, it was gone, nothing there anymore but a hole in the consciousness. *What did you find missing, Reverend Grey, after the break-in? I can't tell, officer. It's missing.*

"Exactly what did the chair look like?" Deedee said.

"I'm not sure anymore. I remember what it felt like, though. It had that cool, dense feel of hundred-year-old oak."

"And Martine dug a gouge in this piece?"

"Not a gouge exactly. More like a little pick. I'm sure Octavian can steam it out or do whatever it takes to fix it."

"Martine is a vandal."

"She was upset."

"Mad at you, you mean."

"People get mad at me," Mother Grey said. "It happens."

The parking lot seemed strangely empty. Something was not in the lot that used to be there. Like her burgled possessions, it took Mother Grey a moment to visualize it.

"Where is the support bus for the California cyclists?" she said.

"They took off right after lunch," Deedee said. "Lock, stock, and nylon tents. Didn't you notice that they were gone from the north forty?"

"Guess I haven't been up that way." Any number of chairs would have fit inside that bus, if one could imagine those wholesome-looking people stealing them. But Mother Grey was more inclined to suspect Father Bingley's party, just on general principles. She pressed her face against the tinted glass of Rodman Sedgewick's black Mercedes-Benz. Nothing seemed to be concealed inside.

"Watch that stuff," Deedee said. "The car is probably alarmed. If it starts hooting, they'll have to send all the way to Vandervliet to get the key from Sedgewick."

"Do you really think he'll sue us?"

"I'd like to see him try," Deedee said.

"Maybe he'll go after Caldwell Gilchrist," Mother Grey said. "Sue him for everything he has."

"Even better," Deedee said. She began to laugh. "Maybe he can sue Caldwell for the Trophette." The Trophette was Caldwell's second wife, slim, blond, Barbie-like, somehow the badge of his success in his father's business. It was only after his father died that Caldwell had dumped Deedee for this woman, whom Deedee did not seem to regard as a fellow human being. "I don't know what he thinks he did to deserve a trophy," she used to say. "Kim must have been the booby prize." The vision of Rodman Sedgewick carrying away the Trophette as the spoils of a killer lawsuit was so droll that it caused Deedee to lose all control of herself. She leaned on the Mercedes, convulsed with laughter. No car alarm went off.

"Get a grip," Mother Grey said. "Help me out here."

"What are you doing?" said Deedee.

"Looking for the lost chair. Here's Sedgewick's car. Nothing in it, as you can see through the windows, except whatever's in the trunk."

"Could the chair fit in Sedgewick's trunk?"

"Good question." She held out her hand at what she remembered was the height of the chair, then mentally turned it on its side and held it up against the car. "It might fit. No telling. As you pointed out, the keys are with Sedgewick in the jail."

Next to Sedgewick's car was Deedee's minivan. No chairs were inside it now, and only Martine could have used it to take the chair away.

No reason why she should do that.

Was there?

"Where were the keys to the minivan last night?" Mother Grey asked.

"What do you mean?"

"I was just thinking, maybe whoever took the chair might conceivably have stolen the keys to the minivan and used it to take the chair away."

"Before we get into that, I feel I must point out that the monastery hasn't been searched yet. What's this panel truck?" Deedee said.

"The brown Dodge van belonging to Miss Newmont. That would be my guess."

"Okay, right." On the side of the truck it said "Newmont Interiors, Rolling Hills," in elegant beige script.

And of course being a panel truck, it could have held a fortune in stolen furniture in the back, concealed under the lumps of gray quilted padding that could clearly be seen by squinting in through the windshield. None of the doors would open, though, so again there was no way of knowing for certain.

The very last thing in the lot was a pale green pickup truck with "St. Hugh's Monastery, Vandervliet-on-Hudson," stenciled on the door. Nothing in the back, nothing in the cab.

And that was it. Either the missing chair was still in the monastery, or it had left with the Californians, or it was in Sedgewick's trunk.

Or it was under the quilts in the paneled van of Miss Newmont. *Interiors? Doesn't that mean furniture?*

That is, unless someone completely unknown to them sneaked in and parked here during the night.

Or, if you wanted to be logical, unless Martine carried the chair into Vandervliet for some reason.

"Let's go inside," Deedee said. "It's starting to rain again."

The lobby of the guesthouse was a scene of as much loud public anguish and confusion as you will ever see in a gathering of Episcopalians. Half the monks and all the remaining guests seemed to have assembled there to bewail the latest turn of events. Mortimer wrung his dishcloth. Jonathan Newmont cracked his knuckles and looked abashed. Father Bingley and his wife were doubly distressed because they had lost their ride home.

"Sedgewick drove us up here," Father Bingley was explaining to Roger Smartt. "Now we have no way to get back to Rolling Hills. He took his keys to jail with him. What shall I do? I have to attend an important meeting in Trenton tomorrow."

Tomorrow—ah, yes, that would be the quarterly meeting of the Department of Missions, the one where he meant to deal the death blow to St. Bede's. Was he angling for a ride in the minivan? *Think again, Bingley.* Five hours in a small space with that man—

"Perhaps Miss Newmont can take you home," Octavian suggested.

But Beryl Newmont refused to take any extra passengers. "From here we're going to a trade show in Buffalo," she said. "I won't be back in New Jersey for weeks."

"Why don't you give them a ride to the train station in Poughkeepsie?" Octavian said.

"No room," she said. "My van is full of merchandise."

Deedee said, "You could unload the merchandise, ferry the Bingleys to Poughkeepsie, and then come back and load it up again."

"There would be nowhere to sit. Furthermore it's raining," Beryl Newmont said. "The things in my van are extremely valuable, some of them almost priceless. I can't let them get wet. Why don't you ferry the Bingleys yourself?"

"Ferry me," said Delight van Buskirk. "I need to be ferried. I want to go home at once."

Then it became a problem like the one with the farmer, the dog, and the chickens or whatever they were, where the farmer had to take all the animals over the river in a boat with a limited number of places without letting any of the chickens get eaten. The guests wrangled and dithered with such spirit that Mother Grey momentarily forgot Beryl Newmont's remark about the valuables in her van.

Mrs. van Buskirk could not travel alone, and yet she was determined to leave at once. So the Smartts offered to accompany her on the train and get her back home from the station by taxi. But how to get these three to the train station in Poughkeepsie?

To say nothing of Father Bingley and Martha. But no, Father Bingley felt that he should not leave yet, that instead he should go to the hospital in Vandervliet and see about Ouida Sedgewick, his parishioner, who might be dying. Or to the local jail or wherever it was they had put Sedgewick, his patron, in obedience to Our Lord's admonition to visit the imprisoned. Of course he would be more at home in the hospital. Prisons were not his usual element.

"Well then," Deedee said, and Mother Grey could have cheerfully killed her, "you and Mrs. Bingley must come back to New Jersey with us."

Octavian was puzzling it out. "If you can drive a stick shift, Father Bingley, you can take the monastery truck to the hospital."

"Father can't drive a stick shift," Martha said. "But I can."

"We'll take the minivan to the train station in Poughkeepsie," Roger Smartt said.

"Good, Roger," Annabelle Smartt said. "Who will bring it back?"

"I will," Martine said. "I'll drive Mrs. van Buskirk and the Smartts to the train, and then on the way back I can stop in Vandervliet and see whether I can get Christophe released."

These arrangements were pronounced satisfactory by one and all, Mother Grey keeping her reservations about the Bingleys to herself. She would speak to Deedee later. Octavian gave Martha the keys to the monastery truck; she went out to take a practice turn around the parking lot. The Newmonts, the Smartts, and Delight van Buskirk bustled away to collect whatever baggage remained uncollected. The bell rang for vespers, and all the monks glided away.

"Mother Grey, may I ask you something?" Father Bingley said.

"Certainly, Father."

"How do you deal with substance abuse?"

What now? thought Mother Grey. Wild speculations surged through her mind, ranging from the notion that Father Bingley himself might be uncontrollably doing drugs to the idea of Martha as a closet alcoholic. *And why ask me for advice, of all people?* "That would depend entirely on the circumstances," she said.

"You started a chapter of Narcotics Anonymous at St. Bede's, didn't you? I need to know what's required for this sort of ministry. I understand, of course, that Fishersville has always had a much greater need than Rolling Hills—" He groped for words to finish this thought, whatever it might be, and Mother Grey tried not to feel insulted on behalf of Fishersville. Of course there was a drug problem in Rolling Hills. There was more money for drugs in Rolling Hills than there was in Fishersville, at least among the old blue-collar crowd. Bingley had never addressed it.

"I can send you some material as soon as I get back home," Mother Grey said. "Is there some—crisis?"

"Jonathan Newmont smokes marijuana," Father Bingley intoned darkly.

"Indeed." Somehow she was not surprised, but Father Bingley seemed quite upset about it. His parishioner.

"I went to his room to speak to him last night and found nothing but a haze of marijuana smoke."

"Last night?" Deedee said. "You mean, when you got up to go downstairs?"

"Yes. I suppose he was in the bathroom. I would be grateful, Mother Grey, for any help you could give me."

"I'll be happy to help in any way I can," Mother Grey said. "Perhaps the first step would be to talk to him, try to get a feel for the extent of the problem."

"Confront him," said Father Bingley. "Yes. Well, if you'll excuse me I must find my Communion kit to take to Mrs. Sedgewick in the hospital. I hope I didn't pack it in the trunk of Rodman Sedgewick's car." He went out, doing a convincing imitation of the White Rabbit, and Mother Grey and Deedee were all alone.

"Curious. How many guys could actually have occupied the men's bathroom at midnight, do you suppose?" Deedee said.

"And never mention that they had seen each other," Mother Grey said. "It does seem strange. Of course, we know that Sedgewick wasn't where he said he was, since he was downstairs doing murder."

But Deedee's mind was occupied with Rupert Bingley. "Nice to see your friend Bingley so friendly," she said.

"Friendly. Yes. He wants something from me, a leg up on his latest venture in outreach."

"So give it to him."

"I'll have the whole ride home to tell him everything I know about drug and alcohol counseling. Five hours in a minivan with Bingley. Deedee, how could you do this to me?"

"I'm doing it *for* you," Deedee said. "Spend the five hours telling the old plaster how to start twelve-step programs in Rolling Hills while you impress him with the wonderfulness of the parish of St. Bede's. He's bound to come away with some appreciation of your efforts. And he'll owe you a favor."

"What you say is true," Mother Grey admitted. "Forgive me."

"No problem. Let's go to vespers." They went to cut through the library, and there, leaning against a bookcase, they found Fergus.

An icepack was on his head, and a dribble of blood ran down his neck. He looked like death.

"My word! What happened?"

"They got the tape," he said.

"Who did?"

"Don't know. Somebody hit me, as you can see. I didn't see who it was."

"Oh, dear," Deedee said. "Now we'll never know what was on it."

Fergus tottered over to the morris chair and collapsed. "I saw what was on it," he said.

"You did?"

"I did, but I can't say I know what it was." He put his head in his hands and groaned.

"Well, what did it look like?" Mother Grey prompted.

"One thing at a time," he said. The women forced themselves to be quiet, and Fergus gathered his strength to tell the story.

"First of all, I took the tape to the common room. We have a VCR there, as you know; one of the women in the Society donated it to St. Hugh's some years ago."

"And you played the tape," Mother Grey said.

"Let me tell it," Fergus said. "Mortimer and a couple of the brothers were in there watching a tape of an old movie—*The Return of Topper,* I think it was—so I had to do some fast talking to get them to let me play my tape instead."

"Okay," Deedee said.

"Then I thought, maybe they don't want to see what's on this tape. I myself was somewhat apprehensive about what it might show."

"My word," said Mother Grey. What could shock this monk, who routinely viewed photographs of slaughter in the killing grounds of Africa and Asia? Of course, a movie of the murder of his friend.

"We loved Basil, you understand. I thought, what if the tape shows him being killed?"

"And did it?"

"When I started it up, it looked like a movie of an empty bed."

"Odd."

"Mortimer and the others were so bored that they got up and left the room. They were rather surly about it. Mortimer said he was going to make cookies."

"Was that all there was on the tape? A view of an empty bed?" Mother Grey asked.

"Oh, no," he said. "Not at all." He took a deep breath and let it out slowly, then took his ice pack and shifted it more to the left.

"In the beginning," he continued, "I thought maybe it would turn out to be something lewd. There was a lot of black and white snow when I started it up, the way it always looks when nothing has been recorded, and then a bedroom appeared, as I said; it looked to me like one of the guest rooms at the monastery. No one was there; nothing was happening. There was just barely enough light to see that the camera was focused on the bed. By and by I noticed the clock."

"Did it show the time?"

"Yes. It was a digital clock with a glowing red readout, the brightest thing in the room actually; every second it changed, which was what drew my eye to it. Nothing else was moving."

"What time was it?"

"Do you know, I don't remember now." He put his hand up to the ice pack, tentatively. "A bit after midnight, I think."

"Wonderful the way those little cameras can pick up images with practically no light at all," said Mother Grey.

"Wonderful," said Fergus.

"Anyway, then—" Mother Grey coaxed.

"Then seven or eight minutes went by, and finally—ooh!"

"Do you want me to get you a Tylenol?" Deedee said.

"Thanks, I just had one."

"Finally what?" Mother Grey said.

"Someone came in."

"Who?"

"At first all I could see was a change in the light. Then a pale shape came into the picture. The lens of the video-camera adjusted—you could hear it making noise, a kind of clunking sound—and I saw that it was a big man, dressed in some light-colored, voluminous garment."

"Was it Sedgewick in his bathrobe?" Deedee said.

"Yes."

"What did he do?" Mother Grey said.

"He sat on the edge of the bed."

"And after that?"

"More time passed. I could hear him breathing. He looked at the door, looked at his watch, looked at the door again, and waited. Then he scratched himself in a few places, looked at his watch, looked back at the door, then looked at the clock.

"A few minutes went by.

"Finally he got up and left. I remember that the time on the bedside clock was twelve-sixteen. And then, when the clock said twelve-nineteen—"

"What?"

"Nothing. Something hit me. When I came to, the VCR was empty, the tape was gone, and some horribly nasty talk show was playing on the TV."

16

Saying he thought he'd better go lie down for a while, but not to call a doctor, he'd be fine, Fergus retired to the monks' quarters.

"Sedgewick must have sneaked in and hit him," Deedee said.

"When?" Mother Grey said. "He was right there in front of us almost the whole time. And more to the point, why? That tape was his alibi for the murder of Basil."

"It was, wasn't it?"

Ah, despair! Mother Grey saw that justice was about to miscarry, all because of her blind, foolish animus against Rodman Sedgewick! "My word, Deedee, we've made a terrible mistake. We sent an innocent man to jail." She thought of Sedgewick locked up in a pen with smelly felons, all on the say-so of herself and Deedee. In her mind she saw his face, peering through the bars, wearing that same snarl. It wasn't bad temper after all, that ugly expression, but righteous wrath.

"And yet he fought like a demon to keep anyone from seeing the tape," Deedee pointed out. "He must be guilty of something."

Still, it made no sense to Mother Grey. "But what was the point of making such a tape to begin with? Nothing happened in it, except that Rodman Sedgewick sat on a bed, all by himself, and did not kill Brother Basil."

"Maybe he faked the tape to give himself an alibi."

"Then why did he try so hard to get it back?"

"Someone else made the tape. Fergus said it was a good view of the bed," Deedee said.

"So?"

"So whatever the action was supposed to be, it was expected to take place in the bed."

"By whoever set up the camera."

"Right."

"That would be Jonathan Newmont, boy cinematographer." She imagined the youth gleefully rigging the thing up, expecting to capture—what? "Was it Jonathan's bed, then?"

"What would Rodman Sedgewick be doing sitting on a young boy's bed in the middle of the night?" Deedee asked. Rhetorically. The fact was, neither of them could imagine.

"Let's find Jonathan and ask him," said Mother Grey.

They went upstairs. Jonathan's room was empty, all cleaned out. In the room next door, everything was packed except the clock, whose red eye winked at them.

"St. Columba. Isn't this the sister's room?" Deedee said.

"Beryl Newmont's room. Right." It began to make more sense, in a sick sort of way. Setting up a camera to photograph a man in his sister's bed.

"But nothing happened in that bed," Deedee said, reading her thoughts again.

"That's why Sedgewick wanted to suppress the tape," Mother Grey said. "He was supposed to meet Beryl Newmont in her room at midnight, and he got stood up, right there in front of God and everybody."

"Go call the police," Deedee said. "Tell them what fools we've been. This is not the sort of knowledge we want to sit on."

"Why don't you call them?" Mother Grey said, somewhat testily. Confessions of foolishness did not spring readily to her lips.

"Wait a minute. I think I've got it." Deedee pulled out her notebook and made a few more notes. Then she tore a page out and handed it to Mother Grey. "Have a look at this."

Mother Grey experienced a sudden pang of foreboding. "Deedee," she urged, "get on with it, my dear. This is the moment where we are the only ones who know for sure that Sedgewick is innocent. Go downstairs right away and call the police. There's a pay phone in the vestibule."

"But first look at this and see whether it makes sense to you."

"I'll look at it while you make the call." She took the paper and glanced at it; Deedee's chart, completed at last, with the little doodles of monks dancing across the top of it.

"Meet me in the gift shop," Deedee called over her shoulder. "My things are all packed. I want to buy a couple of books and then take off as soon as Martine gets back with the car."

"Sounds good to me," Mother Grey agreed. She herself was all packed too. Had she made up her bed with clean sheets? She couldn't remember, with all the confusion of this dreadful day.

No, she hadn't. She would do that now, and then have a look at Deedee's work, which covered both sides of the sheet of paper and would require a certain amount of thoughtful analysis, she was certain. With luck it would not be necessary for her to get out the paper dolls again. Mother Grey folded up the paper and put it in her pocket.

She glanced out her window into the parking lot. Martha Bingley had what looked like a length of hose in her hand; she was down on her knees in her flowered dress, monkeying with the green truck.

Downstairs in the guesthouse Father Bingley wandered aimlessly around, waiting for his wife to get the truck started. It was out of gas, she had said, but she was going to find some somewhere. He left it in her capable hands. After one last trip to the refectory to stock up on a snack for the road, he went into the library. There he found young Jonathan Newmont, all by himself, sitting away off in the corner on an old teakwood chest. Mindful of his resolve to tackle the boy's drug problem, Father Bingley approached him.

For a moment Father Bingley thought he heard thumping noises coming from the chest, but on closer inspection he perceived that the boy was beating on it like a drum, nervously, in rock 'n' roll rhythm. Drug addiction. A terrible scourge. And here was Father Bingley's chance to grapple with it, toe to toe, for the soul of this unwholesome child.

I will confront him, he thought. *Confrontation is said to be a good tactic.*

"Jonathan!" he called. The boy jumped as though startled, but continued his annoying drumming. "I've been meaning to speak to you, Jonathan. I have recently become aware . . ." How to put this? He had never charged anyone with drug use before. Yet it was clearly his duty.

"You've become aware," Jonathan repeated. How shifty his eyes were.

"I want you to know, young man, that I know what you were doing last night," he said.

"You do?" He was drumming with his feet now; his hands were still.

"The love of Jesus Christ is all-embracing," Father Bingley said. "He came into the world, you know, to save sinners."

"So they tell me," the boy said warily.

Back in his study in Rolling Hills was a list of phone numbers that Father Bingley in his innocence had thought never to need, numbers of rehabs and support groups. "You are not alone in your struggle, my son. I want you to know that the Church is here for you, that we offer support in your time of need. There are twelve-step programs—"

"For what I was doing last night?"

"At midnight."

"I was takin' a, um, I was in the bathroom," the boy said.

"You were smoking marijuana."

"My sister made me do it."

A young Adam, blaming the woman. "Temptation must be resisted. The coercion of others is no excuse."

"She makes me do everything."

"I want to see you as soon as you get back to Rolling Hills, my son. There is help. My door is always open."

"Cool," the boy said. He started drumming with his hands again. Father Bingley went on about his packing and gathering, wondering whether he had actually made contact; something about the boy's manner was so strange and preoccupied that he couldn't be sure.

Mother Grey went to fetch the clean sheets and pillowcase from the hall closet. As her hand touched the cool, smooth, ironed cotton, something—the caffeine of her afternoon coffee, perhaps—kicked in suddenly, and her dormant powers of thought began to revive.

She ran all the way down to the gift shop. Deedee seemed to be rummaging behind the counter for a book.

"I've got it!" Mother Grey exclaimed.

She thought she heard Deedee give a muffled grunt.

"What was on the tape shows that Beryl Newmont has no alibi," she said. "She must have tried to poison Sedgewick because he could confirm that she had no alibi. Beryl came here to the monastery on purpose to steal the Harvey Ellis chair and replace it with a forgery, and when she found Basil carrying it away to his room, she grabbed the nearest sharp instrument, Delight van Buskirk's knitting needle, and killed him."

The stooping figure stood up, and it was Beryl Newmont, not Deedee.

"Duh," Beryl said. "Way to detect, Mother Grey. But you've got the story all wrong."

How embarrassing. "I have?"

"It was Basil who was stealing the chair. He had it up on his back and was heading for the monks' quarters, where we couldn't go. Naturally I had to stop him—"

"By stabbing him in the back," Mother Grey said. "An aged monk. Brave deed."

"In the back, naturally. His back was turned to us."

"Ah, of course. What else was there to do? He's in your way, so stab him in the back. After all, there's money to be made."

"You must understand how important it is to me to get that chair. It isn't only the money. I've been planning this for many, many months, ever since I saw the picture of it on Rodman Sedgewick's campaign poster."

"And here we all thought it was him you were interested in."

"He thought so too, the stupid old fart."

And what of Delight van Buskirk's strange vision, two monks carrying Our Lord on a throne? "You and Jonathan dressed yourselves as monks in dark robes. It was you Mrs. van Buskirk saw carrying Brother Basil's body outside in the Harvey Ellis chair."

Beryl Newmont shrugged. "Who knew when we were packing that the real monks wore white?" Then almost as an afterthought, she sprang at Mother Grey's throat.

For someone so slight, she had a surprisingly strong grip. *Modern young women work out,* Mother Grey reflected, trying to counter the strength of her arms. They struggled, lurching into a display table. Plaster crucifixes fell to the floor with a loud crash.

Now surely Brother Mortimer will turn up with his broom and save me. Beryl Newmont was trying to get her hands around her neck. *There's a way to break someone's grip. You push against the thumbs—*

Footsteps approached. Through the door, carrying a coil of rope, a can of paint thinner, and some rags rather than a broom and dustpan, came not Brother Mortimer but young Jonathan Newmont.

17

She was in a coffin, and she was not alone.

This can't be death, thought Mother Grey. It was very different, at any rate, from what she had been led to expect. No bright tunnel, no welcoming arms of Jesus, no crowd of loving spirits of those who had gone before. Where was Granny? Where was Stephen? There was only this dark narrow space and someone crushed up against her, the smell of sweat, the smell of teakwood.

She couldn't move. She could scarcely breathe. Something was in her mouth. Someone was crushing her. Then the smell of mineral spirits, bitter, strong, and getting stronger, and the sound of dripping. . . .

Father Bingley was delighted to see that his little talk with Jonathan Newmont was already bearing fruit. The erstwhile idle wastrel had taken up the work of the monastery and was helping the good monks by polishing furniture.

But he was doing it in a dangerous fashion. It was hard sometimes for young people to grasp the correct techniques, Father Bingley understood that, but still the boy must know that smoking was not allowed in the monastery.

"It's not a good idea to light matches around solvents," Father Bingley pointed out to him. The boy jumped, startled again, and the burning match trembled in his hand before he blew it out.

"Sorry, Father," he said. "I must've forgot."

"In any case I don't think you're doing much for the finish on this chest," Father Bingley said. "Whatever you're using seems to be making it duller."

"Hey, you're right, Father," Jonathan said. "I'll go get some other polish." He took his rags and his can of solvent and headed back toward the kitchen.

Father Bingley watched him go and then turned his attention back to the sorely abused chest. Not only had the solvent dulled the finish, it was standing in pools on the top. You would have thought he was getting ready to set fire to it on purpose.

A folded paper lay next to the chest. Funny, he hadn't seen that before. It was almost as though it had come out of the chest somehow, in the moment when Father Bingley's back was turned.

He picked it up and unfolded it.

Across the top of the page was a long doodle, a line of dancing monks in white robes and black. Beneath the monks was a sort of chart, labeled "The Critical Half-Hour." The chart read as follows:

The Critical Half-Hour

In which we explain what everyone saw, heard, and felt between midnight and twelve-thirty, the approximate time of Basil's murder.

12:00 Berry and Jonathan smoke a joint in Jonathan's room, waiting for quiet in the guesthouse. (Clue of the smell.)

12:04 Berry and Jonathan go downstairs and out to the truck to get the fake chair. (Two black monks, creeping. Does anyone see them?)

12:05 Delight van Buskirk gets up to go to the bathroom.

12:06 Basil, in white, and Christophe, in black, bring the empty chest down to the guesthouse library. (One black monk, one white monk, carrying chest. Delight sees them. Positive sightings.)

12:07 Bingley gets up for a snack. (White monk creeping.) On his way past Jonathan's room, he smells the joint. He looks in and finds no one there. (Negative clue. Jonathan is not where he belongs.)

12:08 Brother Basil goes to the kitchen and eats the last muffin, leaving Christophe resting in the library. (One white monk, creeping.)

12:09 Bingley sees Christophe sitting in the library. (Positive clue. One black monk, sitting like death.)

12:10 Rodman Sedgewick gets up and sneaks into Beryl Newmont's room (one sneaking white monk), only to find that she isn't there. (Negative clue.)

12:11 Bingley rushes back upstairs. (White monk, rushing upstairs.)

12:11 Christophe rushes back to the monks' quarters in order not to be seen again. (One scuttling black monk.)

12:12 Ouida wakes up and finds Roddy gone from their bed. (Negative clue.)

12:13 Roger Smartt puts on a monk's white robe and creeps into his wife's room for kinky fun. (One sneaking white monk and a lady.)

12:13 Ouida sees Roger in his habit, going in Annabelle's

door. (Positive sighting.) She takes him for Roddy.

12:14 *Martha Bingley hears the Smartts making noises. She remarks on it to Rupert, who is now back in bed.*

12:14 *Brother Basil tries to take the real Harvey Ellis chair back to his room.*

12:15 *Berry and Jonathan find Basil making away with the chair. Berry stabs him in the back.*

12:16 *Rodman Sedgewick goes back to his room. (One sneaking white monk.)*

12:17 *In the bathroom, as though in a dream, Delight van Buskirk sees Berry and Jonathan carrying the body of Brother Basil away in the real Harvey Ellis chair. (Positive clue: Two black monks and a white apparition.)*

12:18 *Delight goes back to her room. (One old lady.)*

12:20 *Berry and Jonathan go back to their rooms. (Two sneaking black monks, parting.)*

Strange.

Was this supposed to make some kind of sense? He read it through again. It appeared to be someone's suggestion for a solution to the mystery of Basil's murder. But who had written this? Where had it come from?

It seemed almost as though it might have come from inside the chest while his attention was elsewhere. He tried the lid; it was firmly locked. "Hello in there," he said. No one answered.

So the paper must have been lying there the whole time. But what was its significance?

Father Bingley thought, *I'll go and find Fergus and give it to him.*

18

Brother Fergus was not in the chapel, nor yet in his office, nor in the kitchen, nor was he anywhere upstairs. The guesthouse seemed curiously deserted. The doors of the empty guest rooms stood ajar; gray light slanted into the hallway. Had everyone gone home?

A swish of robes, a patter of feet around the corner. For a prickly instant Father Bingley thought, *The Death Angel.* He could almost see it before him, black with huge wings.

But it was only Octavian.

"Where is Fergus?" Father Bingley said. "I must speak with him."

"Fergus is lying down," Octavian said.

"Will you take this and give it to him for me?" Father Bingley asked. "It's someone's idea of a solution to the murder. Maybe he can figure out what it's worth. I have to go to town to see about Ouida Sedgewick."

"Where did you get it?"

"Downstairs on the floor next to Basil's chest."

"That was really bright, Jonathan."

Mother Grey, still pressed against what she now realized was Deedee, woke to hear voices. She was not dead, and neither was her friend, whose plump chest rose and fell with breathing. Bumping along, they were being taken somewhere.

"Really bright. What gave you the idea to burn down the monastery?"

"I thought if I set fire to those women in the chest, they wouldn't tell on us."

"It's a good thing you didn't try it."

"Why?"

"Because for one thing I wouldn't want to burn up all that great mission furniture. Think what it's worth. Think what it will be worth in another ten years."

"You mean we're gonna come back for it?"

"I wouldn't rule it out," she said. "Roddy Sedgewick is going to take the rap for the murder of that old monk. We'll still be welcome here." Mother Grey heard a match scratch, and she thought of the flammable solvent whose reek still all but gagged her. Other smells could be detected now, and she considered them, one by one, in order to take her mind off the idea of being accidentally burned alive by these people. The smell of herself and Deedee, of course, squashed together in this small space; the smell of truck exhaust, very faint but still detectable; a greasy, linty smell, reminiscent of moving vans, probably quilted padding; and a trace of the unmistakable smell of antiques, a pungent blend of wood, lemon oil, and mouse urine.

Then a whiff of marijuana.

"What I was thinking of," Beryl said, after perhaps holding her breath for a time, "was hiring a big truck and a couple of strong backs. We could take all that stuff away in the middle of the night while the monks are sleeping. Their doors are never locked."

"Cool. But what about these ladies in the chest?"

"We get rid of them as soon as we can."

"Here's an idea," the boy said. "We can drive the van up to that big cliff we passed on our way here and push it off with them in it. The whole thing'll go up in a big ball of fire. Whoom! I could even film it."

"Push the van off the cliff?"

"Yeah."

"This van? The one we need to drive home in? The one with our furniture in it?"

"Oh, yeah. Right."

"And forget taking pictures. I don't want to see myself committing murder on *America's Funniest Home Videos*."

Mother Grey felt Deedee poking her; she must be coming around. She poked her a little bit in return.

Beryl was still thinking, and Mother Grey did not like the turn her thoughts were taking. "I like your idea of throwing them off the cliff," she said.

"How about setting them on fire?"

"No, you moron. It's dark, or haven't you noticed? Everyone on the East Coast would see us."

The road must be winding severely. Buffetted from side to side, Mother Grey began to feel her old car sickness on top of everything else.

"So what do we do, then?" Jonathan said.

"We drive to the top of that mountain up ahead and drop them over Hopeless Cliff, chest and all, into Bottomless

Gully. If anything is left of them after that, no one will ever find it."

This plan was unacceptable. Resistance was called for. Mother Grey arched her back, pushing against the lid of the chest as hard as she could. Alas, it didn't budge at all. When Deedee groaned in pain, she left off pushing.

She twitched her fingers around, trying to get a purchase on her bonds, or Deedee's. No luck.

Surely there's a way out of this.

Fergus rose up on one elbow. The resulting nausea and vertigo were not as bad as they had been the last time he tried to get up. He read the paper through again. Beryl Newmont, that little thing with the hair. Who would have thought it?

"This is my sister's handwriting," he said to Octavian. "Where is she?"

"I can't find any of the guests," Octavian said. "They've all made their beds and flown."

"Who's doing the gift shop?"

"We closed it. Ouida Sedgewick was supposed to be handling it, but she seems to have taken poison; they carried her away in a helicopter while her husband was arrested and put in jail."

"Nobody told me this." The room began to spin again.

"You weren't exactly available. Fergus, are you all right?" Octavian put his hand to Fergus's forehead, feeling for fever. "I think I should get you a doctor."

Carefully, carefully he sat upright and put his feet on the floor. "I'll be all right in a few hours," he said. "I believe I'm concussed."

"What happened?"

"Someone hit me."

"Does it hurt much?"

"No, I just feel dizzy and sick. It will pass off." He read Deedee's timetable through again. So Sedgewick had been arrested? None of this made any sense. "Where did Father Bingley get this?"

"Downstairs on the floor of the library, beside Basil's chest."

His feet found his shoes, and he got himself somehow to a standing position. "Let's go have another look at this chest," Fergus said. But when they got downstairs to the library, the chest was gone.

Presently Mother Grey felt the forward momentum of the car decrease and heard the engine sputter and die. The car rolled to a dead stop.

"What is this?" Beryl snarled. "I know I had plenty of gas."

"Look at that. The needle is on empty," Jonathan said.

Martha Bingley, bless her. Mother Grey remembered seeing her fooling around the monastery truck with a hose and a pail. She must have borrowed gas from the Newmonts' truck; she must have taken all of it.

"Now what?" Beryl said.

"Roll backward and park the truck in the weeds. We can carry the chest up the hill by hand and throw it over the cliff," he said. "It's not far. After that we can go look for gas."

"Not far? How can you tell where we are? It's so dark out there, I can't see a thing."

"I remember that little waterfall running under the culvert. I remember seeing it just after we came over the top of the hill. Come on. We'll each take one end. Then we won't have to worry about these women anymore."

There was a gritching noise as Beryl set the brake, then the sound of the doors in the back opening, and the feel of the shocks swaying as the two Newmonts climbed into the panel truck. Mother Grey and Deedee felt themselves lifted up and heaved over the back end. They dropped to the roadbed with a very uncomfortable bump.

I wish I could get this rag out of my mouth.

Deedee was no doubt wishing the same thing. It was strange to be locked up in a chest with her loquacious friend and not to hear her giving vent to her feelings. Poor Deedee, what would she have to say when they got out of the chest? Presuming that they got out alive.

But of course they would get out alive. Mother Grey turned over plans of escape in her mind. They were more like daydreams, really, for they all seemed to hinge on the work of some outside agency to save them. In one of her ideas a fierce animal came out of the woods and scared the Newmonts into dropping the chest and leaving. In a related fantasy Christophe got loose from the jail and impersonated an African lion, roaring and grunting at them. After the Newmonts ran away, he happened to have a key to the chest, where he had himself spent so much time.

Or they would stumble over the Smartts, making love in the weeds, who would jump up and save the helpless clergywomen. But no, the Smartts were on a train to New Jersey.

Okay then, maybe the lid would pop open somehow and Mother Grey and Deedee would put stones in the chest and run away while Berry's and Jonathan's attention was elsewhere. The Newmonts would continue to struggle up the road, carrying a chest full of stones, and throw that over the cliff.

Or, here was a good one. Maybe an antique dealer from Fishersville would drive by and see them with the chest and would stop to offer them money for it, a chest full of clergywomen. Overcome by greed, they would take it.

Thus Mother Grey amused herself as their captors toiled up the hill. By the smooth swaying of the chest in time with the regular sound of their feet on the gravel, she guessed that the Newmonts were keeping to the road. As for her futile daydreams, none of them came true; neither animal nor human appeared to rescue them. After a while she found herself getting cold, even beginning to shiver, her muscles jerking painfully against the ropes.

The Newmonts did not speak, except every once in a while, when Beryl would say, "Where is it, then?" and Jonathan would say, "Right up ahead, I'm sure it's around the next bend."

At least Deedee was warm, or at any rate warmed Mother Grey. Every so often she poked and jabbed at Mother Grey in a futile attempt to communicate. Mostly it was just annoying, so she jabbed and poked her in return, telling herself it was to let her know that she was still conscious.

At last they stopped going forward and bumped down on the ground. Both Newmonts sat on the chest. Mother Grey could hear their labored breathing.

"Now what?" Beryl said. "You told me it was right up here."

"I thought it was," Jonathan said.

Over the hill in Vandervliet, Detective Francis X. O'Rourke in his warm bed was dreaming about his deceased father. Every now and again old Aloysius O'Rourke came to his fifth son in a dream and spoke kindly to him, taking him fishing or giving him career advice about staying in law school and not becoming a policeman. O'Rourke had loved his father, and he found these visits comforting, even the part about his job. His dead father didn't really expect him after all these years to ditch his job. It was just one of the things he always said.

The other thing he always talked about was how he had smuggled himself into the port of Philadelphia and lived there for fifty years, out of the eye of the immigration authorities, playing his melodeon in bars, working as a bricklayer, drinking, marrying a wonderful girl from Sligo, raising a large family of U.S. citizens. It was a good life.

He wasn't hurting anybody, dodging the law, he always insisted; he wasn't taking jobs from citizens. Nobody else in Philadelphia wanted to lay the goddamned bricks, or anyhow that was what Aloysius always used to tell his boys.

"So what about this little black kid?" O'Rourke's father said. His voice was so clear that he might have been standing right next to the bed, so real that O'Rourke woke up.

It was still dark. No one was in the room except O'Rourke's wife, snoring lightly.

What about the little black kid, then? O'Rourke thought about him in his orange jailhouse jumpsuit, thinner even than Aloysius in his wedding picture, his eyes bigger. Illegal immigrant.

What would happen if, like Aloysius, this kid were to slip through the cracks and disappear into the general populace? First of all, he wouldn't have to go back to Liberia and have his head cut off. That would be good.

But what about after that? What was the worst that could happen? He would take somebody's job? Some citizen?

The phone rang. O'Rourke reached over his sleeping wife to pick it up. It was the night desk clerk at the police station.

"We thought you would want to know," she said. "Those monks called. They think somebody has kidnapped a couple of women up there."

So the Newmonts couldn't find Hopeless Cliff, or at any rate it was farther away than they thought. (Could that be its real name? And how would Beryl Newmont know the names of these local places? No, Mother Grey decided, the girl was being witty. No time like the present for a joke. Hopeless Cliff. Bottomless Gully. Good one.)

"I don't think I can carry this thing any farther," Beryl said.

"Why don't we just leave it here?" Jonathan said. "We could throw those weeds over it."

"Oh, sure, right here by the side of the road. And we can sign our name and address to it while we're at it. What are you, stupid?"

"We could roll it into the bushes."

"I don't think so," she said. "Come on. Pick up your end. Get busy."

But neither of them moved. Then Mother Grey heard a car approaching and saw its lights glimmer through the holes in the chest. The engine slowed. Was it coming from the monastery or from the village? Had they, in fact, been missed? Were they being sought? Maybe it was her antique dealer!

She cocked back her knees, preparing to kick on the chest to attract attention. In vain. The car's engine sped up again, the sound of it fading in the distance. Mother Grey was shivering again.

"In any case we can't stay on this road," Beryl said. "Somebody is sure to see us."

"Who was that who just passed?" Jonathan asked.

"I don't know. Just someone from the village."

"Did they see us?"

"Maybe," Beryl said.

"Look, there's a sign. There's a hiking trail right beyond those trees. I bet it goes up to the cliff," Jonathan said.

"You want to go hiking in the mountains after dark?"

"I have this flashlight. I can hold it in my teeth."

"Oh, all right. We'll try it."

"Like we have a choice."

"Shut up and lift your end."

"It'll be a lot easier coming down," Jonathan said.

The Newmonts picked up the chest again and started up what Mother Grey presumed was the trail to the cliff. Mother Grey willed herself to get heavier. Mothers had told her that toddlers could do this trick; a single toddler could gain fifty pounds, it was said, when it didn't want to be picked up and carried. She suspected that this was one of the gifts that fled with early childhood, like mental telepathy and the ability to learn languages without pain, but perhaps her efforts were bearing fruit. The Newmonts were stopping more and more often to rest.

But more was needed. Soon they would reach the top of the cliff, no matter how many rest stops they might be forced to take. "There it is," Jonathan said. "About fifty yards up ahead."

The chest tilted more and more steeply. They must be hiking straight uphill. Time for bold action! Mother Grey and Deedee began to rock, kick the chest, and hum as loud as they could.

The Newmonts put the chest down.

"Shut up in there," Beryl said, "or else I'll let Jonathan set you on fire."

They picked up the chest one last time. Mother Grey commended herself and Deedee into the hands of God.

And God came through.

Which is to say that it started to rain. Big drops, slow at first and then faster, fell on the top of the chest. They heard the drops; they felt the chest lurch, then lurch again, as Jonathan's feet slipped on the wet trail.

He cursed. There was a dropping and rolling sound as

the flashlight fell—from his mouth? Did he really carry it in his mouth?—and clattered into the distance.

"Let's put it down," said Beryl.

Deedee hummed at Mother Grey, "Mm-hmm." By the grace of God, she knew that what Deedee meant was "On three," and so they swayed, gently at first, one, two, and on *three*, the two of them lurched with all their might toward the same side of the chest, wresting it from the uncertain and slippery wet grip of the Newmonts.

Then the chest began to travel.

The thwarted shrieks of the Newmonts faded into the distance as the chest plunged down the hill, sometimes bumping, sometimes sliding, sometimes falling free. Mother Grey forgot her cold and her terror of burning as she banged and skidded, down, down, toward she knew not what end. At last their wild progress slowed, slowed, and halted. Deedee grunted; Mother Grey grunted in return; they both wiggled a little, and Mother Grey sensed a certain instability in their situation.

The chest had come to rest somewhere other than on solid ground. It was balanced on something. But what? Where were they? Mother Grey wiggled her head around to try to look out of one of the holes. The chest then teetered and fell, a longish drop followed by a splash.

The chest had slipped off the trail and into a mountain stream, whose icy torrent carried them down with ever-increasing velocity, so that it was like a ride, one of those horrible rides where your stomach leaps into your mouth and then they spray you with cold water. It would have been satisfying to scream, but they were still gagged with rags.

The chest began to break up.

* * *

"Aren't you feeling well, dear?" Martha said.

Bingley said, "Yes, I'm fine."

"You didn't eat very well." It was true that the quick bite they got in the hospital cafeteria was somewhat smaller than his usual supper, and equally true that he had left half of it on his plate. Now as they headed back over the lonely road to the monastery, he felt, let's face it, hungry, but he also felt the shadow of death.

Of course, no Christian fears death. To go home to Our Lord is devoutly to be desired. Still, if he were to die tomorrow, what would Martha do? She would have no one left to cook for, and no one to manage the practical day-to-day tasks of the household—the manly ones, that is, changing the storm windows, buying the liquor. Why, she hardly knew how to balance a checkbook. And there was his work at St. Dinarius, unfinished. Unfinished.

For instance, right now he was feeling the call to address the problem of drug abuse. The Newmont boy was doubtless only the tip of the iceberg. Rodman Sedgewick had told him many times, among the other things he constantly told him, that drug abuse was on the increase among our country's youth, and while Sedgewick laid the responsibility for this at the door of the Democrats, Father Bingley was coming to believe that the Church also had a place in correcting the problem. Sedgewick had never pointed to anyone in the parish, anyone within Father Bingley's reach, to say, "That person is abusing drugs," to give his statistics a human face. Father Bingley knew it was out there, but he couldn't grasp it.

Now he had Jonathan Newmont. If the Lord granted him a few more years, he could make of the boy an entire rehab program, better than the one Mother Grey ran, since he was just naturally a better priest, let's face it. Sedgewick would give him money for the project, when he passed his current troubles.

Mother Grey did not have a corner on outreach.

With this thought in his mind, Father Bingley drifted off almost into sleep, lulled by the sound of the truck engine and the gentle sweep of the curving road. He then had something like a dream: He and Mother Grey were before the throne of God, contending over which of them was best doing His will in the world, and Father Bingley found himself saying to the Lord God, "If her work is more worthy than mine, let me die, then, and let her live and continue; but if mine is more worthy, leave me here to do my work, and take her."

In waking life Father Bingley knew perfectly well that you shall not tempt the Lord your God, but in his sleep he had forgotten, for a moment, and by the thundercloud that gathered on the Lord God's brow, he knew it to be a serious lapse. "Aah!" he cried in terror, and woke himself.

"What is it?" Martha said.

"I was asleep."

"Poor Rupert, you need a glass of milk and your own warm bed."

"Cold in here."

"See if you can find the controls for the heater, dear. I'm watching the road. These woods are so wild. Any second I'm expecting a herd of deer to jump out in front of us."

Father Bingley was expecting something too, no less than swift divine retribution for his dreaming behavior. He had heard that some people could tell when their death was near. Did it feel like this? A shiver passed through him. The truck's headlights groped into blackness; trees and big rocks seemed almost to jump at them from the side of the road. He prayed, a prayer for strength, a prayer of silent apology. *I didn't mean it.*

Then as the truck rounded one more bend in the road, a coffin bounced up over a culvert and came sliding across its path. Martha wrenched the wheel of the Isuzu; they swerved aside and went crashing into the ditch.

A moment of frightening silence, and then Martha's voice: "Rupert, are you all right?"

"Yes," he said. It was not his time to die, after all. How else to explain that the shock of this experience didn't kill him outright? His heart was hammering, but it did not fail him.

The door on his side was wedged against the bank. Martha unlatched the driver's side door. It took the strength of both of them to push it open, and then they helped each other climb out onto the road.

Father Bingley limped over to the roadside to inspect the apparition that had caused them to crash, brightly lighted in the headlights of the wrecked truck. It was, yes, a coffin. Part of the lid had broken off.

Staring out of the hole in the lid was the face of Mother Lavinia Grey.

19

Mother Grey looked up into the friendly eyes of Martha Bingley. "Poor things," Martha said. "What happened to you?" As she undid their ropes and gags, Father Bingley stood in the road and counted his bruises. "How you're shivering!" Martha said. How they all were shivering! "Rupert, check the truck and see if there are any blankets in it. Are you all right, dear?"

"I think I'm cut," said Mother Grey, easing her weight off Deedee.

"Badly?"

She looked at her arm; it wasn't deep. "No."

"Me neither," said Deedee. "I'm fine." She didn't look fine, sitting shivering on an old stump, but they could get checked in detail when they reached some sort of shelter. A roof. A fire. Blankets. Even a drop of whiskey would not go amiss. Mother Grey wondered whether the monks kept such things.

"No blankets here," Father Bingley said. "How about that other truck? Maybe they have blankets."

The truck he spoke of turned out to be the Newmonts' van, parked across the road on a flat place in the weeds.

"Oh, dear," said Martha. "I'm afraid that's the Newmonts' panel truck. I had no idea they would try to leave so soon."

"You took their gas, didn't you?" Mother Grey said. She jumped up and hugged her. "You know, you saved our lives, Martha. They were carrying us up the hill to kill us."

"Good heavens," said Martha Bingley.

"Their gas?" Father Bingley said. "Is that why you wanted to buy extra gas in the village?"

"Yes, to pay them back."

Father Bingley opened the driver's side door to the panel truck. "Nothing wrong with the battery, at least," he said, as the interior lights came on. "And look here! They left the keys in the car." He honked the horn twice.

"What are you doing?" Martha said.

"Calling the owners. We have gas for them."

"Dear, they're killers. They were going to murder these women. I'd just as soon they stayed in the woods."

"Oh, right. Of course."

Mother Grey helped the shivering Deedee into the back of the Newmonts' truck, where they found a pile of quilts, oily with furniture polish. "Wrap yourselves up while I put this gas in the car," Martha said as she emptied the can of gas into the tank of the panel truck. "Then we'll get out of here as fast as we can. You too, Rupert, cover up. You're shaking."

Father Bingley took a blanket and huddled in the passenger seat. Mother Grey could hear his teeth chattering, or maybe it was her own, or Deedee's. Suddenly there was a rushing sound, something coming through the woods and down the hill at them. Everyone flinched, but it was nothing but a herd of deer. The graceful creatures sprang across the road one by one and disappeared into the bushes.

The engine started handily. As they headed back for the monastery, Mother Grey and Deedee each got naked under her greasy quilt and piled their wet things in the corner. It felt good to be dry. One quilt wasn't even enough, actually, Mother Grey decided, and she snatched another from over a piece of furniture, lying against the side of the van.

And there was the Harvey Ellis chair. Dark as it was in the back of the panel truck, Mother Grey could tell it by the feel and the smell alone. "Eureka," she said softly.

"Eureka," Deedee replied. It was almost the first word she had spoken since their strange ordeal.

"How are you?" Mother Grey said.

"If I had known how we would spend this evening," said Deedee, "I would have taken a shower this morning."

"Think nothing of it," said Mother Grey.

"Very well. As to how I am, I've been better," she replied, "but I do believe now, after everything is said and done, that I will live."

Having warmed up her tongue, at least, Deedee resumed her normal habit of chattering, even insisting on telling them all an old Irish story, one that she had learned, so she said, at her sainted mother's knee.

"It had to do with a funeral party in Donegal. The horse-drawn hearse was toiling up the hill to the cemetery when a terrible storm arose, with thunder and rain, and a great bolt of lightning struck at the very feet of the horse, causing it to rear back. So the back of the hearse flew open. Out went the casket, corpse and all, and slid back down the hill."

"Did this really happen?" said Father Bingley.

"Are you doubting my mother, Father? So here's the funeral party with the hearse continuing on, all unknowing, and the corpse going back down into the town."

"What town?" said Father Bingley.

"I believe it was Creeslough. Maybe you heard of the incident. Anyway down the hill it went, into the village, across the road and through the window of the apothecary shop."

"My heavens," said Martha.

"The druggist behind the counter was so startled that he said, 'May I help you?' and the corpse—"

"Yes?" said Mother Grey.

"The corpse sat up and said, 'Can you give me somethin' to stop me coffin?'"

20

At the entrance to the monastery parking lot, O'Rourke and a small band of policemen came at them out of a cold rain; Martha Bingley rolled the window down to see what they wanted, and they stuck drawn guns in her face.

"Where are the clergywomen?" O'Rourke demanded.

"Right here," she said. "I'm bringing them back, you big bully." When she started to cry, Mother Grey and Deedee crowded up into the front seat to comfort her, clutching the furniture padding around their nakedness.

"She's had a perfectly awful night," Mother Grey said to the detective, who was already beginning to realize these weren't kidnappers. "Crashing a truck, saving our lives—"

"I'm sorry," O'Rourke said. "Park the truck and come inside."

Fingers too numb to dress themselves, Mother Grey and Deedee went up to St. Dymphna with Martha, where they took hot showers and allowed her to help them into dry clothes. It was an unfortunate oversight on the part of the architect who planned St. Hugh's that it had no fireplace. The four chilled travelers were reduced to gathering around the open oven door in Brother Mortimer's kitchen, rubbing themselves and trying to bring life back to their hands and feet.

"We aren't still going home tonight, are we?" Deedee said.

Father Bingley said he didn't want to take a long drive tonight.

"But my dear," Martha said, "what about your meeting tomorrow? Didn't you tell me you had an important vote to cast?"

"They'll have to cancel the meeting until next month," said Father Bingley. "Without me they won't have a quorum." Mother Grey's heart leaped; she would have an entire month to straighten St. Bede's affairs and pay the diocesan assessment before the Department of Missions convened again.

As soon as they had eaten something and warmed themselves, O'Rourke came and asked them questions.

"So where are the Newmonts now?"

"On the mountain, wandering around without a flashlight," Mother Grey said. "Watch out for them. They may be unarmed, but they're nasty."

"They won't get far. I have a crack team of mountaineers to track them down."

"Really?"

"No, not really, but I do have a couple of guys who know the trails. Meanwhile we'll cruise around to the local householders and tell them to keep their doors locked. Trust me, they're as good as in custody."

"And Rodman Sedgewick. What about him?" Mother Grey asked.

"We let him out an hour ago. He's at the hospital with Mrs. Sedgewick. She's out of the woods, by the way."

"Do you think he'll ever forgive us?" she said to Deedee. "I feel awful about sending him to jail the way we did, an innocent man."

"Look at it this way," Deedee said. "Whatever he suffered, at least he didn't get tied up, gagged, stuffed in a chest, and rolled down a mountainside in a freezing rainstorm."

"Good point," she said, sticking her hands back into her nice warm armpits.

Octavian put his head into the kitchen. "I don't suppose," he said, "that you saw anything of the Harvey Ellis chair."

Mother Grey told him it was in the Newmonts' panel truck. He rushed out into the night, reappearing shortly in the front hall, tenderly carrying something wrapped in gray quilting.

He put it down and whisked the wrapping off. There stood the chair before them all; the interesting proportions, the quaint and cunning details, the lamplight glinting off the metal inlay, the wood grain's deep glow. It all looked subtly different, more significant somehow, now that the chair had become an object to kill for.

"Good as new," Octavian said, caressing it. Then he frowned. "Except for this tiny dent on the arm."

"It's worth a lot of money, isn't it?" Fergus said. "I suppose we could sell it if we had to."

"Someone offered me thirty thousand for it two years ago," Octavian said.

"Is that all? You mean Basil was killed for an object

worth a mere thirty thousand dollars?" Fergus was near tears.

Father Bingley said, "It wasn't the money. He was thwarting that woman's plans, standing in her way. You know how it is with the truly wicked." Mother Grey thought it an acute observation, coming from Father Bingley, and for an instant she was tempted to revise her opinion of his intelligence.

But everyone knew what wickedness was: implacable, blind self-will. The real question was, what was goodness?

Or more precisely, would Father Bingley persist in his efforts to close St. Bede's, even though he thought of himself as a virtuous person? Or would he come to understand the wickedness of his course of action, before it was too late?

They would tackle him in the car and bombard him with five hours of propaganda.

Octavian could not take his eyes or his hands off the Harvey Ellis chair.

"Why don't you take it to your cell?" Fergus said. "Keep it safe. No one will bother it there."

"I couldn't," Octavian said. "It belongs to the guesthouse."

"I'm a guest," Deedee said. "I say take it."

"All right, I will, then." He hoisted it up on his shoulder and was gone.

It was getting close to time for the Great Silence again, when Martine came in. Father Bingley and Martha had gone up to bed by then, leaving Mother Grey and Deedee, the chill gone from their bones at last, to drink hot tea in the refectory with Fergus and Mortimer.

The chef jumped up when Martine came in, tired and wet, and offered to get her some cold chicken.

"I ate in town," she said. "But thanks."

"Did everyone get away okay?" Deedee asked.

"Yes, I put the Smartts and Mrs. van Buskirk on the train in Poughkeepsie. The train left before it started raining, but the drive back to Vandervliet was pretty bad. It's freezing all over the roads again. We aren't going to try to drive tonight, are we?"

"No, but we'll get away tomorrow morning first thing," Mother Grey said. "While you were gone, we had something of an ordeal. You don't have to be anywhere tomorrow, do you?"

"I have to get back to Newark and clean out my desk," Martine said.

"Why don't you just blackmail Sedgewick into giving you and Albert your jobs back?" Deedee suggested. "Now that you know his secret."

"No," she said. "In the first place we don't want to work for him. And in the second place he'd probably just have us killed."

"Will that be before or after he sues Deedee and me for everything we have or ever will have?" said Mother Grey.

"That reminds me," Fergus said. "I have something for you." From somewhere in the depths of his clothing he drew forth a videotape.

"What's that?" Deedee said. "Sedgewick sitting on the bed watching the clock? No, thanks, I—"

"No, no. This is the other videotape, the one we took of Sedgewick and Octavian fighting. Take it," he said. "Make a couple of copies. Its very existence should take the edge off Mr. Sedgewick's enthusiasm for frivolous litigation."

"What are you saying? That I should use it to blackmail him?" Deedee was aghast.

"I would never say such a thing. Just remind him what a fascinating presentation it would make on the evening news, in case he brings an action against you and Mother Vinnie for causing his false arrest."

"I saw our friend Sedgewick at the jail in Vandervliet," Martine said. "He was on his way out. I gave him a card."

"Your card?"

"No, not my card, a card for the National Association of African-American Trial Lawyers," she said. "It has the phone number. I suggested he might want to join."

"What did he say?"

"He said, 'Aaargh.' "

"As well he might," Mother Grey said, "now that his boys are macaroons. They say that Ouida is making a good recovery from whatever was in the coffee."

"I distinctly saw him give her that coffee," Deedee said.

"So did I," Mother Grey said. "But maybe one of the Newmonts gave it to him first. Do you think—I don't know—do you think he'll run for office as a black candidate?"

"He won't get my vote," Martine said. "But then, he never did. Tell you what, I'm just going to forget everything I know about that man. In fact, I'm going to forget I ever met him."

"It works for me," said Mother Grey.

"That's if he gives me a really good reference," Martine said. "Of course, I'll leave the usual letter to be opened in case of my death."

"Good move," Deedee said. "And what about Christophe?"

"I didn't find him," Martine said.

"How is this possible?" Mother Grey said.

"He wasn't there. Detective Francis X. O'Rourke stood right there at the front desk and told me to my face that he had never seen or heard of anybody called Christophe."

"What!" This was outrageous.

"They said they had no record of his arrest. As far as O'Rourke is concerned, he doesn't exist. I guess they let him go for some reason. I'm worried about him."

"Don't be," said Fergus. "He's here."

"Then that explains the message O'Rourke gave me," Martine said. "He said to tell you, Brother Fergus, that somebody better get out of St. Hugh's, because other people might make mention of him in a report. If they come looking for him, he'd better not be here."

"That message seems pretty clear," said Mother Grey.

"We could take him with us when we go," Deedee said. "Set him up in a wood shop in Fishersville. You should see this kid's work, Martine. He makes the most beautiful chairs."

"Albert has some woodworking tools," Martine said. "We could put him in the room over the garage. It's all winterized."

"Go and ask him if he wants to come with us," said Mother Grey. Mortimer went to fetch him.

Christophe came in, dressed in jeans and a short-sleeved shirt, showing his strong arms and capable craftsman's hands. He was scarcely recognizable without his habit.

"So I'm to leave here," he said.

"Only if you want to," Fergus said.

"I probably should. Detective O'Rourke warned me to start packing when he dropped me off here. I said, 'What shall I do? Where shall I go?' and he told me I might go to Philadelphia and lay bricks," Christophe said. "I don't know what he meant. I know nothing of bricks."

"Would you like to come to New Jersey?" Martine said. "My husband and I have an extra room over the garage. I think you could be comfortable in Fishersville."

"Comfortable?"

"Yes, come with us. We'll set you up in a workshop and

find you some customers," Mother Grey said. "There's a thriving market there for art furniture."

"There will still be a bed for you here," said Fergus. "When the, ah, heat is off."

"Thank you," Christophe said, and to the women, "You are leaving when?"

"First thing tomorrow," Deedee said. "We'll say good-bye now, since we'll be leaving at dawn, before the Great Silence is over." They all hugged.

Mortimer came out of the kitchen with a bulging brown paper bag. "Take this for the road. God bless you," he said, and then he was gone. In the bag they found half a loaf of homemade bread, sliced and buttered, and a bunch of bananas.

The Great Silence fell.

Before dawn the police found Beryl and Jonathan Newmont sheltering in the wrecked monastery truck. Jonathan confessed everything in exchange for a hot cup of coffee and dry clothes, while his sister screamed obscenities at the arresting officers.

The sun was shining and the red buds were showing on the trees as Deedee, Martine, Mother Grey, and the Bingleys took the long road back to New Jersey. A skinny black kid in jeans and a ski jacket went with them, sitting silently in the corner of the backseat, while Martine and Deedee chattered about the excellent works of Mother Grey at St. Bede's in Fishersville. Martha, at least, was listening to them; every so often she said, "That's wonderful," or, "How nice."

The deep spirit of peace that ruled over the monastery seemed scarcely to have been ruffled even by the terrible events of the weekend. Mother Grey and Father Bingley felt it still, in spite of everything, and for at least as long as the homeward journey lasted, they tried to like each other. They really did.